PENGUIN BOOKS

KHUSHWANT SINGH'S
BIG BOOK OF MALICE

Khushwant Singh was India's best-known writer and columnist. He was founder-editor of *Yojana* and editor of the *Illustrated Weekly of India*, the *National Herald* and the *Hindustan Times*. He is the author of classics such as *Train to Pakistan*, *I Shall Not Hear the Nightingale* (retitled as *The Lost Victory*) and *Delhi*. His last novel, *The Sunset Club*, written when he was ninety-five, was published by Penguin in 2010. His non-fiction includes the classic two-volume *A History of the Sikhs*, a number of translations and works on Sikh religion and culture, Delhi, nature, current affairs and Urdu poetry.

Khushwant Singh was a member of Parliament from 1980 to 1986. He was awarded the Padma Bhushan in 1974 but returned the decoration in 1984 in protest against the storming of the Golden Temple in Amritsar by the Indian Army. In 2007, he was awarded the Padma Vibhushan. Among the other awards he has received are the Punjab Ratan, the Sulabh International award for the most honest Indian of the year and honorary doctorates from several universities. He passed away in 2014 at the age of ninety-nine.

Khushwant Singh
Big Book *of* Malice

PENGUIN BOOKS

An imprint of Penguin Random House

PENGUIN BOOKS

USA | Canada | UK | Ireland | Australia
New Zealand | India | South Africa | China | Singapore

Penguin Books is part of the Penguin Random House group of companies
whose addresses can be found at global.penguinrandomhouse.com

Published by Penguin Random House India Pvt. Ltd
4th Floor, Capital Tower 1, MG Road,
Gurugram 122 002, Haryana, India

 Penguin
Random House
India

First published in Penguin Books by Penguin Books India 2000
This edition published in Penguin Books by Penguin Random House
India 2019

The views and opinions expressed in this book are the author's own and the
facts are as reported by him which have been verified to the extent possible,
and the publishers are not in any way liable for the same.

The *Hindustan Times* and the *Tribune* have kindly given us permission to use
their columns 'With Malice Towards One and All . . .' and '. . .This Above All'
respectively. All except the following columns have appeared in 'With Malice
Towards One and All . . .':

'Nose-picking', 'Why bookshops are important', Bribing journalists', 'Shobha
De and gender wars', 'On losing a friend', 'Politics divorced from morality', 'The
inimitable R.K. Laxman', 'Kakar's *Ascetic of Desire*', 'Garbage called astrology',
'The one and only Nirad Babu', 'Prepare for death while alive' and 'Dog-haters
and astrologers'.

ISBN 9780143450030

Typeset in Sabon by Digital Technologies and Printing Solutions, New Delhi
Printed at Replika Press Pvt. Ltd, India

www.penguin.co.in

Foreword

I have never taken any person or event too seriously, least of all myself. I have always been a nosey person forever probing into other people's private lives. I love to gossip and have an insatiable appetite for scandal. Forty years ago when I landed my first job as editor of *Yojana,* I discovered I could exploit these negative traits in my character to my benefit. Readers were amused by what I wrote and asked for more. An editor of the *Times of India* who carried the burden of the country on his head scoffed at me as he remarked, 'You have made bull-shit an art form.' I was flattered.

I resumed my column when I took over as editor of the *Illustrated Weekly of India* in 1969. I wrote on subjects other editors considered beneath contempt. I wrote on why some monkeys have red bottoms, on the refined art of bottom-pinching, shop-lifting without being caught, the joys of drinking, mocking politicians, godmen, astrologers. Above all, name-droppers were my favourite target. I had great fun writing these columns and evidently people enjoyed reading them. My friend Mario Miranda designed the logo putting me in a bulb with a pile of books and a bottle of whiskey beside me. It has become my trademark. My colleague Bachi Karkaria who helped me write some of my better pieces summed me up in three words: sex, Scotch and scholarship. I found the third untrue but flattering.

After I was sacked from the *Illustrated Weekly,* I carried my column to the *National Herald,* then to *New Delhi* and finally to the *Hindustan Times.* When my contract for editorship of the *Hindustan Times* was terminated, I was asked by the proprietor K.K. Birla to continue writing my weekly column on a freelance basis with permission to syndicate it. That proved to be a bonanza. Now my two columns 'With Malice . . .' and '. . .This Above All' are picked up by papers all over the country in both English and regional languages. They bring me dough and notoriety. I hope this compendium brings more of both.

Khushwant Singh

Nose-picking

It is a nauseating habit most of us indulge in, when no one is looking. Tolstoy was forthright in his condemnation: 'People who pick their noses and dispose of the pickings on the undersides of the dinner table are not likely ever to see God.'

So, few of us are likely to be let in the Pearly Gates and have *darshan* of the Almighty. Charles Darwin, author of *The Origin of Species* found this one distinguishing factor between us and our simian cousins. 'Monkeys do not pick their noses,' he wrote. 'This is about the only disgusting personal human habit at which they are not also adept.'

Who in the world would have thought of writing a book on the subject except an American! So one has—a Yank by the name of Donald Wetzel. My friend Amir C. Tuteja (Punjabi-turned-US citizen), who lives in Washington DC and periodically sends me off-beat literature, included *The Nose Pickers' Guide* (Ivory Tower Publishing Co.) along with two others, *The New York City Cab Drivers'*

Joke Book which I will write about later in this column, and *The Fart Book* about which I will not say anything lest it creates a stink.

A new word you may like to add to your vocabulary is 'booger'. It is the stuff you extract out of your nostrils. They are of two kinds: dry boogers and wet boogers. Whatever kind they be, you instinctively try to stick them on the sides of the chair you are sitting on, or under the table. If you happen to be out on a walk, you stick them to the sides of your trousers. Beware of depositing them on your bed head-rest because the king of shrinks, Sigmund Freud, declared that 'People who put their nose pickings on the pillow case are sick.'

Donald Wetzel has drawn a list of many varieties of boogers. In the dry variety are marble, buck shot, black hole, dry hairy (firmly attached to a large hair in the nostril), smoky bear and pygmy.

Then there is the phantom which does not really exist except in your imagination and you go on probing for it in your nostrils endlessly till somebody screams at you to stop.

There is also a bastard booger which refuses to be moulded into a disposable shape and sticks to your finger no matter how much you try to get rid of it. Similarly, wet boogers have many sub-species: fish-eye, pizza, elastic, chicken turd etc.

Two aspects of nose-picking should be noticed. First is that few people dig for them in their nostrils with handkerchiefs. Most people enjoy the exercise using only their index fingers. Oscar Wilde wrote 'Show me a man who picks his nose with his pinky and I'll show you a man with a nose like a rabbit.'

The other noticeable aspect is that the habit of nose-picking is far more prevalent among men than women. Queen Victoria remarked, 'If one would remain a lady or gentleman, one must thoroughly wash one's hands after picking one's nose.' Her Britannic Majesty was not a nose-picker and was not amused if she caught any of her courtiers probing their nostrils with their fingers.

4 March 1995

Why bookshops are important

I have a rough-and-ready yardstick to measure the quality of life of towns and cities. On the positive side are the number of schools, colleges and bookstores they have; on the negative, the number of cinemas and restaurants. But the ultimate litmus test of a town's sophistication is the number of bookshops it has, the kind of books they stock and the customers they draw.

Stores that cater to students selling school and college textbooks do not count. It is others which have books on fiction, poetry, science, technology, philosophy, comparative religion and general knowledge, and the kind of people who buy them.

I am heartened to see that though prices of books keep going up, book-buying is also on the increase. Bengalis have always been book buyers. The day they receive their salaries, they go to buy their ration of reading for the month. *Dal-bhaath* and *maacher jhole* are second priority. People of other states are picking up the habit.

Punjabis, who are at the bottom of my list as book buyers (top of the list of consumers of beer and tandoori chicken), are turning more bookish. I had evidence of this recently at Chandigarh.

The Capital Bookstore, which is a leading bookshop in the city, had the bright idea of inviting authors to meet their patrons and autograph their books for them.

Upamanyu Chatterjee *(English, August)* drew a stream of admirers and signed away scores of books. I did not do as well. Many people came simply to gape at me and made me sign books by other authors. However, Capital Books found the exercise commercially viable.

15 April 1995

Bribing journalists

Nothing new about it: ever since the first newspaper was published, attempts were made by politicians and businessmen to keep proprietors, editors and reporters on their right side. The best way of keeping people on one's right side is to periodically grease their palms. As the press grew in size and became the most powerful moulder of public opinion, governments, industrial houses and ambitious politicians devised ways and means to keep media persons happy.

Since the central and state governments are the largest advertisers, they disburse their patronage in different ways: selective disbursing of advertisements, subsidized housing, invitations to accompany prime ministers and presidents on foreign tours, nominations to state councils or the Rajya Sabha, invitations to tour states to publicize development projects or sites of tourist interest, awards etc.

Industrial houses likewise place advertisements in papers which support them; withhold them from those which do not. Ambitious politicians get round media persons by entertaining them or giving them gifts. Within limits these means of keeping media people happy did no great harm and did not sully the image of Indian journalism very much.

However, in the last decade or so, chief ministers have become more blatant in their dealings with the press, and press people more shameless in accepting largesse and writing false reports in favour of the hands that feed them.

It was left to Mayawati, chief minister of Uttar Pradesh, to expose how much her predecessor had done to corrupt the media: outright grants of cash running into lakhs of rupees to editors, correspondents and reporters from his discretionary quota; paying their medical bills, out-of-turn allotment of cars, scooters, cooking gas and telephones.

The image of the Indian press as a purchasable commodity has sunk to the lowest. I recall the comments of the owner of a tavern which was largely patronized by prostitutes. He gave drinks and meals to newspapermen at half rates. When asked the reason he replied, 'Commercial courtesy to an allied profession.'

Although I have been in journalism for almost forty years, since I did not write much on politics, no attempts were made to bribe me. Of course I received a lot of invitations to cocktail parties and dinners and was invited by foreign and state governments on non-official visits and entertained right royally. No one offered me cash or gifts.

Like most others in my profession, I got a bottle of Scotch or two on Diwali or New Year's Eve and at times some readers sent me a basket of mangoes or *matthees*. I accepted them gratefully because I did not regard them as bribes. The final test of whether or not a journalist has been bribed is what he writes about the people from whom he has received gifts.

I have never let small gifts or flattery affect my judgement. For me, a bewitching smile is more corrupting than a crate of premium brand Scotch. I am very much like foolish English media men:

You never hope to bribe or twist,
Thank God! an English journalist.
But knowing what the fellow will do
Unbribed, there is no occasion to.

9 September 1995

With more sorrow than malice

A week before Christmas, the temperature dropped low enough to give us an excuse to light a fire in the sitting room. There is something very romantic about an open fireplace which electric radiators cannot match. The cheerful crackle of wood followed by the silent glow of embers of coal does something to the human soul. They evoke nostalgia for the days of long ago. In my case, of pre-Christmas days in England when I went round with English boys and girls singing carols at neighbours' doorsteps—'Silent Night, Holy Night', 'Hark, The Herald Angels Sing', 'The Holly and the Ivy' among others; of people once loved who have gone out of my life—either dead or estranged.

It was not so much the personal past that occupied my mind this Christmas. It was what had happened to my country in the year drawing to a close. I turned over the leaves of my diary in which I record daily events: What I did, names of people who died, earthquakes, floods, fires, rail disasters, election results, changes of governments etc. I wanted to give 1995 a name which would depict most of what happened. I decided to label it the year of Chandraswami. To me, Chandraswami symbolizes the worst in our national character: saffron cloak and beard—the traditional garb of renunciation camouflaging pursuit of worldly wealth and power, befriending arms dealers, utilizing call girls, manoeuvring empty-headed politicians and civil servants, hiring criminals to eliminate critics. More distressing than his personality was the fact that he continued to wield enormous influence and received homage from hundreds of thousands of his countrymen and women.

I suspect it was the immoral atmosphere created by the acceptance of men like Chandraswami that paved the way for the resurgence of religion-dominated parties like the Shiv Sena, VHP, and BJP: they made good showing in the elections. They also revealed their total disregard for commitment to political principles. BJP factions ditched the BJP; Telugu Desam ditched Telugu Desam, BJP ditched Mayawati. Letting down their allies of yesterday carried no odium.

We groped in the dark looking for leaders who would, by example, show us the way.

That was not to be. Jayalalitha indulged in a wedding extravaganza unparalleled in the history of recent times. Far from reprimanding her, to the prime minister's grand daughter's wedding, 25,000 guests were invited. None of this vulgar display of power and opulence took place during the times of Pandit Nehru or Indira Gandhi. What happened to the Guest Control Order which forbade inviting more than fifty guests?

In a society which overlooks small misdemeanours, people begin to think they can get away with anything. So thousands of crores were made in kick-backs, thousands of crores given by businessmen to ministers and senior politicians—no accountability whatsoever.

When wheeler-dealers in black money go scot-free, there is little to deter men with violence in their blood doing what they will. So we had Naina Sahni hacked up and dumped in a tandoor, and Chief Minister Beant Singh blown up with a dozen others by a human bomb. In a climate of violence, crimes like murders, rapes, robberies and thefts went up steadily.

Will these trends continue into 1996? Unless we get an avatar who will descend from wherever he lives to redeem us from evildoers and restore the rule of righteousness, I am afraid they will.

30 December 1995

Laloo and the Tigress

By strange coincidence, on the very day the chief minister of Bihar, Laloo Prasad Yadav took a bunch of flatterers to task, Sheba, the Royal Bengal Tigress in Alipur Zoo in Calcutta, killed a young man who tried to put a garland around her neck, and severely mauled his companion. Laloo's flatterers had set up Laloo Fan Clubs, Laloo Vichar Manches, the Laloo Sena, Laloo Brigade, Laloo Free Health and Education Centre, etc. Animals are not prone to flattery, and as Sheba showed, have more effective ways of dealing with sycophants than we humans. All Laloo could do was to impose fines on his unwanted, unwelcome *chamchas* while Sheba slew one and maimed the other: left to herself, she would have gobbled up both. Laloo has yet to learn that flatterers resemble friends just as much as wolves resemble dogs. We would like to know what Laloo did to the snivelling bard who composed the Laloo Chalisa eulogizing his qualities of head and heart. I don't know if he has read any Shakespeare. He should heed the warning in *Julius Ceasar*, where a courtier speaks about his boss thus:

> *'but when I tell him he hates flatterers*
> *He says he does; being then most flattered.'*

Laloo's denouncing flatterers will prove counter-productive because it will generate another breed of bootlickers who will laud his condemning flattery. It is wiser to be like a duck: treat flattery like water—swim above it, dive in it, but don't let it wet your wings. Adlai Stevenson, in my estimation the ablest politician-statesman of recent times, put it neatly: 'Oh, flattery—it's like a cigarette; it is all right if you do not inhale the smoke. If you do, you can get lung cancer.'

Flattery comes in many forms: the more devious, the more difficult to resist. Most often, the fellow who claims to speaking his mind *('Main to seedhee seedhee baat karney wala hoon')* and mixes in a few harsh words to establish his bona fides, is the more difficult to

resist and the most poisonous. People in positions
of power, as Laloo Prasad is, should presume
that no one will ever tell them the truth about
themselves except their enemies. That is what
makes the *kursee* such a lonely seat to occupy:
you can't trust people who say nice things to
you on your face; and you don't want to hear
unpleasant things from anyone. You have to
cultivate indifference towards both flattery and
criticism: both *(khushamad* and *ninda)* should
leave you unscathed. You have to be your own
prosecutor, defence counsel and judge. It is an
awesome responsibility. Jonathan Swift took a
balanced view of the phenomenon:

> *'Tis an old maxim in the schools*
> *That flattery's the food of fools*
>
> *Yet now and then your men of wit*
> *Will condescend to take a bit.*

Salt on the Tiger's tail

The Nawab of Pataudi was going through a bad patch. In a succession of matches, he went out without scoring a run. Once while playing at Wankhede Stadium in Bombay, his wife Sharmila Tagore rang him up. The secretary of the club replied, 'Madam, the Nawab Sahib has just gone in to bat. I will ask him to ring you back as soon as he returns to the pavilion.'

'No,' replied the Begum Sahiba, 'I'll wait on the line. He never stays at the wicket for very long.'

13 January 1996

Republic Day 1996

January 26 is more than a day for parades, march pasts and flag hoistings. It is the day we adopted our Constitution. So it is proper that on this anniversary, besides watching the grand parade in New Delhi on our TV sets, we ponder on the state of our Constitution, and if we conclude that it is not in good shape, devise ways and means to restore it to good health. We need not look very far back in time to see that it has become very sick. In the last session of Parliament, neither the Lok Sabha nor the Rajya Sabha was able to conduct any business: Crores of rupees spent in getting MPs from remote parts of the country to deliberate on problems facing the nation and suggest solutions were wasted in wrangling, shouting at each other and staging walkouts. The message is clear: The system is not working and we must make a change. The sooner the better.

What should we do? The only alternative is to switch over to a Presidential form of government. Let the entire country elect one man and his deputy as President and Vice-President for a set period—let us say five years—then empower the President to choose his cabinet of advisers from among the ablest talent available in the country, whether or not they are members of Parliament. This would obviate balancing acts performed today to make the cabinet representative of regions and religions. It would put an end to defections and corruption at ministerial levels. It would also be a much cheaper form of government.

The Presidential system would be closer to the one which obtains in the United States, and now with the chances of being saddled with a dynastic succession having receded, it will also be truly democratic.

I have no idea of how we can make the change from the Parliamentary form to the Presidential form without political turmoil. Others more familiar with our Constitution assure me that if there is popular mass support for the change it can be done smoothly. Let us spend this Republic Day pondering over what is best for the governance of our country.

Lodhi Gardens

On the afternoon Lee Kwan Yew, prime minister of Singapore, was due to speak at the India International Centre, I had difficulty in finding a place to park my car. When I entered the park, I was dismayed to see crowds of picnickers all over the place. 'This park does not belong to my father,' I said to myself, 'everyone has the right to enjoy themselves as they like.' So I proceeded on my evening stroll passing groups of between a dozen to one hundred enjoying themselves on the warm winter afternoon. Their main preoccupation was eating and making noise. Well-dressed men, women and children gobbling *samosas, pakoras, mithaee* and washing them down with tea or coffee. Transistor radios blared Hindi film music. They danced and clapped their hands as they accompanied the songs. Children ran around with coloured balloons and tossed shuttlecocks. Boys played cricket using ancient walls of historical monuments as their wickets. Around every group were strewn paper, plastic cups and saucers. One large party had a man issuing orders over a loudspeaker to children engaged in relay races. There were bhelpuri sellers and vendors of tea and cakes. The alcoves on the walls enclosing Sikander Lodhi's tomb had been converted into urinals. The large meandering pond with fountains was covered with green slime. It had not been cleaned for over a year. Every few yards, the stink of sludge used to water lawns and flower beds assailed my nostrils.

This is a park I have known for over sixty years as one of the most beautiful in the world with ancient mosques and mausolea scattered among lush green lawns and flowers. At one time, peacocks and partridges scampered about the verdure. Brown owlets sunned themselves in niches in stone walls. There was a baffling variety of birds: four kinds of mynahs, two types of shrikes, koels, shamas, babblers, kingfishers, woodpeckers, hornbills. Most of them have disappeared because humans with their filthy habits have made it impossible for birds and beasts to live with them.

Singapore used to be as dirty as Delhi. Under Lee Kwan Yew's iron rule, it has become one of the cleanest, greenest, pollution-free garden cities of the world. He realized that some people have to be taught civic responsibilities by the use of the *danda*. In Singapore, anyone caught littering the road, spitting or urinating, will find himself in jail. All it needs to restore Lodhi Gardens to its past glory is to have a magistrate on duty for four hours each on Saturdays and Sundays. He should be empowered to impose heavy fines on the spot on those who throw paper cups and saucers, urinate against walls, use transistors and loudspeakers in the park. Hawkers of bhelpuri and vendors of chai-biscuit have to be ordered to ply their trade with ice-cream sellers at the gates, not inside the garden. It will need only a dozen sweepers to clean the pond of scum and filth. It has to be done with the *danda,* because we do not understand the language of reason and civic responsibility.

20 January 1996

Bhookump

An earthquake of a magnitude hitherto unrecorded on the political Richter scale struck India in the third week of January 1996. So far, only about a hundred politicians and civil servants are known to have been injured. But as the search for bodies lying buried under the debris continues, many more are expected to be dragged out in the days to come. The epicentre of the earthquake has been pinpointed to a very elegant farmhouse in New Delhi's Chattarpur suburb not very far from the historic Qutub Minar. The farmhouse belongs to one S.K. Jain, about whom little is known besides his being a fixer and a middleman with vast sums of money at his disposal. It is alleged that he was able to get cabinet ministers, senior bureaucrats, and politicians belonging to parties antagonistic to each other, to have contracts with foreign firms sanctioned. He can also arrange payments to be made in foreign currencies, thus dodging the Foreign Exchange Regulation Act (FERA) and income tax. These, known as *hawala* transactions, are carried out by word of mouth, and nothing is put down on paper. There was, and is, honour among thieves and law-breakers.

Unfortunately for him and hundreds of others, this Shri Jain was in the habit of noting down illegal payments he made in his personal diary. And more unfortunately for him was the fact that among the recipients of his bounty were terrorists engaged in overthrowing the government. When these gangsters were nabbed, the trail led to the luxurious farmhouse in Chattarpur and the tell-tale diary seized.

What is new about this *hawala* racket is the impressive list of beneficiaries ranging from the prime minister, ministers of cabinet, opposition party MPs and dozens of others. Most people including myself are highly sceptical about the charges made by the Central Bureau of Investigation. Although I have said many harsh things about L.K. Advani's narrow-minded communal outlook, there are two things I will never believe about him—that he can be bribed, or be unfaithful to his wife. I can't say that about any of the others named by the CBI. The other thing that bothers me is why after all these months since the diary was found did the CBI decide to move in on this matter, and why it has been so selective in naming suspects. It is evident that the green signal was given by the prime minister only now. Nobody can believe that he has suddenly come round to the view that the corrupt should be brought to book and the law should take its course. Most people believe he has a game plan and is putting it in operation on the eve of the general elections. What exactly his game is, is known only to himself.

Our politicians have never enjoyed much of a reputation for integrity among the masses. Shri S.K. Jain of Chattarpur has reinforced the commonly held view: *Sab chor hain.*

27 January 1996

Memories of November 1984

The arrest of H.K.L. Bhagat brought back
bitter memories of events of the first week of
November 1984. They were triggered off by
the wicked murder of a gracious lady who
bore no ill-will towards any community (bless
her soul!). But there were thousands of others
who, with murderous cries of *'khoon ka badla
khoon sey leyngey'* (we will avenge blood
with blood), mercilessly butchered and burnt
alive over 5,000 innocent men, women and
children who had nothing whatsoever to do
with the lady's death, but by circumstance of
fate belonged to the community of her killers.
Such things are known to happen all over the
world. For some reason I hoped they would not
happen in the land of Gandhi. And if they did,
the heavy hand of dharma (the law) would fall
swiftly on their necks and they would get the
punishment they deserved. For months nothing
happened. On the contrary, the succeeding
prime minister, Rajiv Gandhi, condoned the
massacre of innocents: 'When a big tree falls,
the earth around it shakes.' Three non-official
commissions of inquiry comprising a retired

chief justice, retired judges of High Courts, retired ambassadors and civil servants (not one of them from the aggrieved community), published names of those they held responsible for the holocaust, amongst them, those of H.K.L. Bhagat (cabinet minister), Sajjan Kumar (MP) and Jagdish Tytler (minister). Not one of them had the guts to take members of inquiry commissions to court for implicating them in murder, arson, rape and looting. They had the protective umbrella of the Congress party and a Congress Government to shield them. The Government went further in appointing its own commission of inquiry under a very amenable Justice Ranganath Mishra who exonerated the Congress party of all guilt. It was left to the Bharatiya Janata Party to bring perpetrators of the November 1984 violence to book. Quite honestly, I do not believe that after the long lapse of time there will be enough conclusive evidence available to convict the criminals.

Their only punishment will be to live the rest of their lives with their consciences—if they have any.

There are many questions about the 1984 killings which need to be answered. First, who gave the signal to the hooligans to 'teach the Sikhs a lesson?' With my own eyes I saw them burn and loot Sikh property while the police on duty in large numbers looked on as spectators. Second, why were orders to impose curfew and shoot at sight never carried out? The looting, killing and arson continued unabated for two days and nights. We now know that army units from Meerut were summoned immediately after news of Mrs Gandhi's death and sporadic violence had erupted. An army unit arrived that very night. It was first halted on the Delhi border. And then ordered to report at Delhi Cantonment. It happened to be the Sikh Light Infantry. Who was responsible for confining this unit to the barracks?

Only one person knows the answers to all these questions. He is P.V. Narasimha Rao who was home minister during those turbulent days. I may add one more question for him to answer: 'Don't you think it is time that those named as perpetrators of the 1984 crimes were expelled from the Congress party?'

3 February 1996

Living longer: Making love to the last

There are no clearly-defined borders between youth, middle and old age. Some young men and women become middle-aged in their thirties, others remain young in their fifties and sixties; some become impotent in their youth; others continue to enjoy sex into their eighties. Indeed, most people will agree that as long as you are capable of enjoying sex, you are young; when the sexual urge disappears, you have become old. Men are more obsessed with proving their potency than women and, when natural impulses begin to wane, will try all kinds of aphrodisiacs to keep going. Unfortunately for them, so far, medical science has not produced any reliable sex rejuvenants. Good health and worldly success are more potent than any *kushta*. Henry Kissinger was hundred per cent right when he said that power is the ultimate aphrodisiac. So we find so many successful politicians compulsive womanizers. Equally potent is the company of the young and the vivacious.

Sexual urges are generated by hormones secreted by the pituitary gland located beneath the brain, the testes, and in the case of women, in the ovaries. These age with the ageing of their owners. Also, in monogamous marriages, the absence of variety (which is indeed the spice of life when it comes to sex) and monotony deprives both partners of the urge to engage in lovemaking. Statistics show that in marriages which have lasted more than twenty years, the sex urge has all but disappeared. Attempts to revive it with the same partner are not successful, but failure to do so does not impair matrimonial closeness. Men in their fifties and sixties are still capable of sex once a week. The urge tapers off in the seventies and is usually extinct in the eighties.

But both men and women hanker after sex even after the natural urge has abated. The natural way to prolong the sex urge are liaisons with younger people. Ageing men are drawn towards girls younger than their daughters and young girls respond to overtures of men who become their father figures. Likewise, older women take on young lovers who see in them their mother-mistresses. The relationships are utterly Freudian, utterly unnatural but utterly fulfilling for both partners even if the sex in the relationships is not satisfactory.

One sure way to impotence is to ignore the presence of attractive members of the opposite sex. Men and women who take to religion in their later lives and spend most of their time in the company of their own age group age prematurely and lose the zest for living.

For those anxious to revive their sex lives, there are hormone injections which revive potency for fifteen days. Most pathetic are cases of men who have the desire but are unable to perform. Even for them medical science has found stuff to inject into their genitals to revive them. Experiments are afoot to produce a pill which will have the same effect.

Heavy drinking over many years can have disastrous effects on male or female potency. Alcohol may temporarily whip up desire, but it will rob the drinker of the power to perform. Fortunately, most drinking men in their late seventies and eighties if given the choice between a willing female and a slug of premium Scotch, will opt for the latter.

10 February 1996

Tidal wave of intolerance

Over the last ten or fifteen years, intolerance of other people's views has been increasing. I have been a victim of this on more than one occasion. During Vasant Sathe's regime as minister of information and broadcasting, I persuaded Doordarshan to let me produce a series of programmes entitled 'The World of Nature' with Sharad Dutt as the director. The series based on flowering bees, birds, insects, mammals and reptiles commonly seen in Delhi proved to be enormously successful. Then I ran foul of Prime Minister Indira Gandhi: she suspected I was in her daughter-in-law Maneka Gandhi's camp. She told Sathe's successor, N.K.P. Salve, that I was getting too much exposure on the electronic media. Salve, who made brave speeches in the Rajya Sabha on the freedom of expression, had me blacklisted.

I could understand AIR or Doordarshan not inviting me to participate in political dialogues, but to prove his loyalty to the PM, Salve put a blanket ban on my appearing on AIR or Doordarshan. 'The World of Nature' which had nothing whatsoever to do with politics, disappeared from the screen. H.K.L. Bhagat, who succeeded Salve, retained the ban. This did not prevent him from telling the world how the Indian Constitution guaranteed citizens the right to speak their minds.

In West Bengal, the minister of culture put a ban on Usha Uthup's shows. Usha does not strip or sing obscene songs—largely Hindi film songs in a style uniquely her own. She is immensely popular with her audiences (I for one, enjoy her singing and traipsing around the floor). The same minister announced a ban on Samantha Fox dancing and singing in Calcutta. Who the hell does the minister think he is to deprive people from enjoying what they like? Is he minister, or commissar of culture? I am surprised Jyoti Basu did not rap him on the knuckles and tell him such things should not be done in a democracy.

Bal Thackeray does not like Salman Rushdie's *The Moor's Last Sigh* because it lampoons him as a tin-pot dictator. He does not take Rushdie to court for libel but his lumpen followers threaten to vandalize bookstores which stock the book: goondaism is more effective than the law.

Thackeray also does not want to let Pakistani cricketers play in Bombay. He is not bothered that others may want to see Indians play the Pakistanis. His storm troopers threaten to dig up the pitch: so no Indo-Pak cricket matches.

Jayalalitha does not like Tamil magazines writing anything critical about her. Those that did, had their offices wrecked. All in the name of the freedom of the press.

In Bangalore, a farmer's union smashed up the Kentucky Fried Chicken outlet sanctioned by the government and cleared by the High Court. Their leader, Professor M.D. Nanjundaswami, proclaims he will never allow it to function. I don't know what this man teaches but he could not be teaching respect for the law or maintaining democratic norms.

Yet another personal experience: Some months ago, I made the most innocuous remark about how I rated Gurudev Tagore as a novelist and writer of short stories. I had Bengali boys who had probably not read anything by Tagore baying for my blood. The Bengal Assembly passed a unanimous vote censuring me. So did the Rajya Sabha. There was not one West Bengal MLA or MP of the Rajya Sabha to protest that every citizen has a right to express his or her views on a writer. Surely everyone will agree with me that this is not a healthy trend in a country like ours which is still striving to become a model democratic state.

Living longer: A healthy diet and pills

In my younger days, while staying with American friends, I used to be amused to see the assortment of coloured pills laid out on their side plates and swallowed in turns with sips of orange juice, tea or coffee. Breakfast was, and is, more health-oriented than other meals. It started with fresh fruit juice or grapefruit followed by cornflakes or muesli to which dried prunes or figs were added. Toasts were of wholemeal bread. It was easy to see that the concern was to keep bowels moving regularly. What the pills were for I was not quite sure. Nor was I sure of what my hosts swallowed after dinner, because they did so in the privacy of their bedrooms. Probably sleeping pills were taken every night.

I no longer find pill-taking as amusing as I used to, because I take at least half a dozen, of different colours, with my breakfast and dinner. With the onset of years, bodily functions become sluggish and need to be stimulated regularly. By middle age, a large number of men and women become somewhat diabetic, have uric acid, blood-pressure problems, and need more than roughage in their food to maintain regular bowel movements. Pills have indeed become important items on our daily menus. We cannot afford to scoff at them.

Everyone has to make his or her choice of pills, depending on what their body needs. My morning begins with a glass of fresh orange juice squeezed the evening before and left in the fridge. That has vitamin C. I follow it up with a mug of Korean ginseng tea. I don't know what ginseng has in it, but I know it does me a world of good. Then I take another two mugs—one of Indian tea with a teaspoonful of sugar and milk, and one mug of plain hot water. I take all these fluids in the morning to get my bowels moving.

My pill-taking is with my light breakfast of
one toast (wholemeal) and a mug of tea (the
fifth of the morning). With the toast, are a
capsule of Becosule, two pills of Trefoli, one
for high blood pressure, one Zyloric (against
uric acid) and a capsule of garlic oil. At
about 11 a.m. I take a mug of hot water with
Marmite. I take another garlic pill each with
lunch and dinner. I don't need any sleeping
pills but do take an after-dinner digestive.
After trying different brands of *choorans*
and Hajmola, I have settled for a little-
known ayurvedic preparation, Sooktyn. The
combination of food and pills keeps me free
of ailments and reasonably fit for my age. I
don't need any tonics but I keep a tinful of
sucking vitamin C tablets which I put in my
mouth whenever I feel under the weather.

The healthiest of foods may still be short
of vitamins and minerals. To make up for such
shortages, it is advisable to supplement food
with antioxidants such as vitamins A, C and E.
They reduce the chances of strokes and heart
ailments, prevent cataracts from developing in
the eyes, even check loss of memory. Available
in the market now without a doctor's

prescription are varieties of multivitamin tablets. It is best to consult your doctor before deciding what to take.

People in their fifties or older should have a thorough medical check-up at least once a year. There are many ailments such as diabetes and high blood pressure which show no early symptoms but strike a person unawares. I had personal experience of this. Having played a vigorous game of tennis in the morning and cleared my desk of pending work, I went to Parliament feeling on top of the world. My friend Ghulam Rasool who sat across the aisle eyed me for a few moments, then got up, grabbed me by my arm and ordered me to follow him. Without telling me, he took me to the Parliament clinic and asked the lady doctor on duty to take my blood pressure. I kept protesting that I was fit as a fiddle and never had any blood pressure problems. The lady went ahead with her examination, and told me 'Your blood pressure is dangerously high. You must see your doctor immediately.' I did. He took a second reading and confirmed that my BP was indeed dangerously high. Ever since, I have been taking a BP tablet every day.

I asked Gulam Rasool how he was able to read trouble on my face. He replied, 'I have lost many members of my family who have had strokes without any prior warning. I can tell high BP by looking into a person's eyes. I saw it in yours.'

17 February 1996

Two days in Jamshedpur

The last time I was in Jamshedpur I spent a few hours at the TISCO guest house in Dimna. A large spread of water encircled by green hills, ancient trees, fresh air, no sounds except the calling of water fowl across the lake. I told Russi Mody who was then chairman of TISCO, that the place should be reserved for artists and writers. 'You are welcome to stay here as long as you like and write whatever you have in mind,' replied Russi. 'We can fly you in from Delhi in our private plane and drop you back whenever you have had enough.' I was never able to avail of his generous offer of hospitality.

This time, Jamshed Irani was sultan of the TISCO kingdom. I approached his begum, Daisy. 'You say your piece at the Rotarians meet and we'll arrange for you to be driven to Dimna. You spend the night there and come back in time to catch your return flight to Calcutta.' That is exactly what I did.

First, the Rotarians meet. After the experience of Lucknow, I had determined never to accept Rotarians' invitations. They are a nice, well-intentioned lot, but awful bores with no sense of punctuality. Jamshedpur was different. It seemed as if they had done up the steel city only for me. It was at its flowering best. Gardens were ablaze with flowers in full bloom: roses and chrysanthemums, the largest and the most fragrant I had seen or smelt for a long time. Bright red salvias and golden marigolds lined the borders. They must have the best gardeners in India. The meeting went along with clock-work precision. The invocation to Shri Ram was mellifluously rendered by Mandira Mukherjee, and the speeches were uniformly first rate. I heard C.R. Irani denounce corrupt ministers by name. I had decided to quote him, but after seeing that

the *Statesman* (which he edits) had nothing to
say of his speech, I too decided not to name the
corrupt. He said he had documentary proof to
support his contentions and the confidence that
they would not dare to take him to court for
defamation of character. He did not spare the
prime minister: 'You want to know when the
elections will be held?' he asked. And replied,
'They will be postponed to the last day because
each day in power means crores of rupees to
these people including the prime minister.' He
went on to affirm that if Manmohan Singh
stood for election from any urban constituency
in India, he would win hands down because
the people know him to be an honest man. But
corrupt ministers (he named them a second
time) would be rejected everywhere because no
one trusted them now.

Irani was followed by retired Chief Justice
B.P. Beri of Rajasthan High Court—a virtuous
virtuoso performance in *shudh* Hindi; oratory
the likes of which Jamshedpur had not heard
for a long time. The star performer of the
afternoon session was Padma Khastagir, the
first woman to become a judge at the Calcutta
High Court. Her speech was full of love and

compassion and exhortation to revive family virtues. I was the last in the list of speakers. Whatever applause I received was due to the introduction made by the very comely Neelam Kumar whom I had never met but exchanged correspondence with.

Back to the haven of peace, Dimna. I retired early to rise before dawn to take an early morning walk along the dam and watch migrating water fowl. The delusion of peace and quiet was rudely shattered by three loudspeakers blasting simultaneously. *'Munda bigrra jaaey'* said one, *'Ooperwala, very good, very good'* blared the second, *'Roop suhana lagta hai'*, sang the third. Buses from Calcutta and other cities began to offload passengers in hundreds. More noise came from transistors. We are indeed addicted to loud noise. I decided to return to Jamshedpur. The picnickers gave me a farewell-kick song. As they guzzled their bhelpuri, the loudspeaker blared: *'Tujhey mirchee lagee to main kya karoon? Theyree naanee maree to main kya karoon?*

24 February 1996

Stray thoughts on *hawala*

Once it used to be said about the Chinese, now it is being said about us: 'There are only two kinds of Indians: those who take bribes and those who give them.' Actually, there are a third and a fourth class of Indians as well. In the third category are those quite willing to accept bribes but are not considered worth bribing. And the fourth who are quite willing to give bribes but do not have the means to do so. I belong to the third of these four categories of Indians. Though quite willing to be bribed, nobody considers me worth bribing because I have nothing worthwhile to give them in return. A little praise in my column is worth no more than a bouquet of flowers and even less, a winsome smile. As the list of those who accepted money from the Jains gets longer and longer and my name does not appear on it, I feel more left out and despondent. In their scheme of values I am not worth a *khotasikka* (a base coin).

There is an Italian saying that money has no colour. In India we have two kinds of currency, one distinctly different from the other: one is

white and the other black. Of the two, it is
the black which is more valuable; it need not
be accounted for, no taxes need be paid on
it, and you can get its equivalent in dollars,
Deutschmarks, francs, pound sterling or yen
without getting clearance from the Reserve
Bank of India. Its greatest advantage is that
if you want any favours done for you, it goes
much further than its white counterpart. That
is why in the transactions with politicians, the
money the Jains gave were all in black and the
recipients must have known very clearly what
the Jains expected to get in return. They were
not one bit concerned with which party came
to power in the states or at the centre, so they
were happy to offer bribes to Congressmen,
BJP, Janata Dal or any others provided they
got their business done. Akbar Allahabadi will
forgive me for parodying his lines:

> *Congress ko bhee salaam, Bhajpa ko
> bhee pranaam*
> *Siyaasat na chaahiye, mujhe dhanda
> chaahiye.*

2 March 1996

Ministerial misconduct

I have so many instances of government
ministers misbehaving with women working
under them or wanting some favours from
them, that I could compile a sizeable collection
of true short stories. Very very rarely do these
women dare to lodge complaints to the police
or inform the press: They know the police will
do nothing and press publicity will tarnish
their own names. All that the misbehaving
minister has to do is to deny the charge and say
it is politically motivated, and get away scot-
free. The few ladies who came to tell me about
their unpleasant experiences at the hands of
ministers did not want me to write about it or
name either them or the minister concerned. So
what was I to do?

In the latest episode narrated to me, the
lady in question is quite willing to be named
and divulge the name of the minister as well.
I decided not to do so to avoid trouble for
the papers that reproduce my column and for
myself. So I will only narrate the incident to
show how crude these Johnnies-come-lately
can be when they occupy seats of authority.

This lady, a dedicated social worker, is endowed with a youthful, shapely figure. All she wanted was to get a clearance of a modest sum of money for a project already sanctioned by the government. People working on the project were too timid to approach the minister—or perhaps unable to get an appointment. They asked the lady to see him on their behalf. Being well-known in the state, she was immediately given an appointment and shown into the minister's private office. She told him what she wanted. She was assured the money earmarked would be forwarded at once. The minister then turned to more personal matters.

'I am told that once upon a time you were an airhostess and a fashion model.'

'I was, sir,' the lady replied. 'That was many years ago.'

'You still hab a bhery good pheegur,' he complimented her.

'Thank you, sir,' she replied.

'Let me see your pheegur,' he commanded.

The lady thought the minister wanted to see how tall she was. She stood up to let him see for himself. 'I am too tall for women of this region. But fashion models have to be tall.'

He was not satisfied. 'Not like this. Properly, without your sari,' he ordered. This time the lady understood what he was after and walked out of the minister's private office.

The money sanctioned for the project was not forwarded.

Magazine glut

When anyone consults me about the prospects of launching a new magazine, I do my best to discourage them. The market is glutted; you will have difficulty in getting adequate advertising support to keep it going; circulations of magazines of long standing are going down rapidly; cable television is stifling the print media; you will be pouring good money down the gutter, and so on. But people who have the itch for editorship—and money to spare—take the gamble. And lose.

Last month there was a clutch of new magazines. First, a lavishly-produced *India Today Plus,* a quarterly at Rs 75 per copy. Aroon Poorie, editor-proprietor of *India Today,* is known to have the Midas touch.

Every venture he takes on, he makes highly profitable. Nobody thought that a fortnightly magazine would make good in India. *India Today* proved them wrong; it has established itself as the top magazine of the country as a journal of reference. It may not be as exciting to read as *Sunday* or the *Week*, but you can't do without it. Then, Poorie went into classical music cassettes, a public school, and an art gallery. All three ventures proved highly prestigious and successful. But I have my grave doubts about the future of his new quarterly. How many Indians will be interested in taking cruises on the *Queen Elizabeth* costing a few lakhs per holiday, or smoking Havana cigars at a minimum of Rs 500 a smoke? And picking India's ten most beautiful women is stale stuff. However, Poorie has plenty of money to throw around.

Outlook (Rs 10) is now a couple of months old. It is edited by Vinod Mehta who has earned an enviable reputation for boldness, innovation and writing lucid prose. What he lacks is stamina. His *Outlook,* though more readable than any other weekly today, may patent into the circulations of *Sunday* and the

Week, but is hardly likely to make a dent in the circulation or prestige of *India Today.*

Then there is *Yellow Top* (Rs 15). It calls itself a 'cabzine' (I don't know what the word means), and claims to be 'the only one of its kind'. That, it certainly is not. It is the usual cocktail of politics, sports, films, food and small talk.

I am more uneasy about the *Scoria* (Rs 20), a quarterly 'for the connoisseur' from Chandigarh. It is devoted to literature: poetry, short stories, essays and interviews. I am apprehensive of its future. My friend Bhupendra Hooja, retired IAS living in Jaipur, took on the *Indian Book Chronicle* some years ago. It has much the same kind of material—reviews, essays, poetry, etc.—as *Scoria.* I know Hooja continues to put his savings into his venture. And now he has launched into its Hindi version *Parakh* as well.

The most daring magazine venture of last month is *Himal: South Asia* from Kathmandu, owned and edited by the Dixits. It has spread its net wide over the whole of the subcontinent and beyond. It is somewhat like the Nepalese version of *India Today,* dealing with politics, economics, social problems, the arts, music and book reviews. The first issue does not carry the price but I would guess it would be around Rs 20. But even the inaugural number does not have enough ads to make it economically viable.

The main problem that all these new magazines face is to develop distinct personalities of their own: they should have things that other magazines do not have. Not many people can afford more than a couple of magazines per month, and few will give up those they are used to reading, by replacing them with something new. However, I wish all of them the best of luck.

16 March 1996

Hai hai cricket!

It is estimated that 600 million people around the world were glued to their TV sets for the month that the Wills World Cup tournament was being played. Every match lasted on an average of eight hours of the day and night. Multiply the two figures and you get the mind-boggling total of how many hours people reduced themselves to being couch potatoes for a month. The vast majority of viewers had never played the game nor intend to do so; for them it was a spectator sport. More disconcerting is the fact that most of them had little knowledge of the skills required for the game, but nevertheless treated winning as a matter of national prestige or something to lay bets on. Who am I to sermonize? I was one of the 600 million monkeys who watched all the matches. And I have never played cricket nor know the difference between silly mid-on or a long slip, between yorkers, googlies or off and on spins. There is something about this game which is as addictive as cocaine or hashish.

Cricket used to be a gentleman's game played by gentlemen and watched by genteel ladies in their Sunday-best saris. It is no longer so. Today, competitive cricket is played by professionals who sweat their guts out to make big money in the few years of their youth and then live on their earnings augmented by fees received as commentators on radio or TV, writing articles for sports columns of newspapers and magazines, or advertising fizzy drinks. Spectators have likewise ceased to be gentle folk (who watch the game comfortably seated on their sofas), but hoi polloi who troop in their thousands to sports stadia armed with whistles, bugles, firecrackers, soda water bottles and missiles to hurl at fielders who come within range. They have no sportsmanship. When one of their batsmen hits a sixer or their bowler gets a wicket, they explode with enthusiastic yells of triumph. When players of the opposing side do the same, they relapse into sullen silence as if *naanee mar gaee* (their mother's mother had died).

Our match against Pakistan which we won, and the one against Sri Lanka which we lost, showed how as a nation we have not grown to maturity and have lost the spirit of sportsmanship. While we were gloating over the breastbeating in Pakistan following its defeat, we did worse when we were humiliated by Sri Lanka. With Pakistan we have a hate-hate relationship; if it is m*aatam* (mourning) in Pakistan, it has to be *jashn* (celebrations) in India. And vice versa. But we outdid the Pakistanis in poor sportsmanship and bad behaviour when the Sri Lankans pulverized our team. So it is not three cheers but two *hais* for Indian cricket.

23 March 1996

The Edwina-Nehru affair

I was the press officer at the Indian High Commission when Panditji came to attend the first Commonwealth Prime Ministers' Conference. For months before his visit, I had occupied a room on the first floor of India House; the copper plate beside the door bore the legend 'Countess Mountbatten of Burma'. My high commissioner, Krishna Menon, who knew which side his bread was buttered, went out of his way to kowtow to people who mattered to Prime Minister Nehru. The Mountbattens were on top of this list. Menon hoped Lady Mountbatten would become a regular visitor to India House. I was under instructions to clear out of the room within five minutes' notice leaving no trace of my having used it. Her Ladyship never entered the room reserved for her. His Lordship did once by force of circumstances: by mistake, he turned up half an hour early for a reception.

I was one of the India House staff ordered to be present at Heathrow Airport when Prime Minister Nehru arrived. It was a cold winter night. We were lined up to be introduced to him. 'What are you fellows doing here at this time of the night?' he asked us. 'Go home and get some sleep.' He was pleased to see us, his minions, assembled to salaam him. At Krishna Menon's insistence, I went to Panditji and asked, 'Sir, will you be needing my service? I am your PRO.' He snapped back, 'What, at this hour? Go home!'

The next morning, the front page of the *Daily Herald* carried a large picture showing a lady in her negligee opening the door to let in Prime Minister Nehru. The caption read: 'Lady Mountbatten's midnight visitor.' It went on to add that Lord Mountbatten was not in London. The press photographer had taken the chance to get this scoop. After getting to know the way Krishna Menon's mind worked, I would not put it beyond him to have tipped off the editor. When I came to India House, he told me that the prime minister was furious with me and I had better keep out of his way for a few days. So I did.

A day before the prime minister was due to return home, he invited Edwina Mountbatten to dine with him at a Greek restaurant in Soho. When the two were seated at a corner table, a battery of press photographers arrived on the scene. Next morning, many London papers carried pictures taken in the cosy basement of the Greek cafe. This time there was no escape. I was summoned to Claridges Hotel. As I entered Panditji's bedroom, he looked me up and down to ask me who I was. I had been with him all of the seven days. 'Sir, I am your press officer,' I replied. 'You have strange notions of publicity,' he said in a withering tone. At the time, it did not occur to him or to me that the only person who could have tipped off the press was Krishna Menon. Menon had a mind like a corkscrew.

However, there seems to be no doubt that there existed some kind of emotional, and possibly, even physical attachment between the Lady and the prime minister. Examine the profiles of the two: You will be startled by the resemblance. There is usually a strong element of narcissism in the choice of one's beloved. But Edwina was by no means the only woman in Panditji's life even while this affair was on. Catherine Clement (author of *Edwina and Nehru: A Novel),* who started her research shortly before Rajiv Gandhi was assassinated, had to wade through more than 11,000 photographs and hundreds of letters to write her book. When asked what she thought of this relationship, she replied, 'Beautiful! It was simply beautiful!'

Happy families

Much has been written about what it takes to make a happy family. It is like casting pearls of wisdom before swine. I can count the number of happy families I know on half the fingers of one hand; unhappy families, by the score. Also, happy families tend to be self-centred, unwelcoming towards outsiders, and uniformly boring. On the other hand, however awkward it may be to visit an unhappy family, you will find a lot of individuality amongst its members (which is why they find it difficult to get on with each other) and they are usually more interesting.

I can think of only one family which was held out as an example of an ideally integrated home. I stayed with them many times. I was always made to feel like an intruder and a poor relation. They spent their time praising each other and running down everyone else. The children, far from growing up into healthy, successful men and women, fell by the roadside as non-entities.

The base of every family is its children. Neglect them, and you erode the very foundations on which the family edifice is built. You achieve the same negative result by mollycoddling them. The family tree is meant to shelter them from the rain and the scorching sun while they are juveniles. Once they are adults, the umbilical cord must be finally cut, they must be exposed to the harsh world, learn to make their own decisions, make their own mistakes and pay for them. But make sure that the nucleus of the family home remains intact so that they can return to it to lick their wounds till they are ready to face the world again.

No one can prescribe rules for a happy family. There must be some kind of bonding like being together at meals, going out together to the pictures or picnics, and if you are believers, worshipping together. I have found that in families which have books in their homes for different age groups, there is usually more interaction between its members, less contention and more harmony. A bookless home is no home. A bookless family is less likely to hang together than one in which members have other things than making money and scandals on their minds.

We all know by experience that families whose members are at variance with each other are the most unhappy because it does not take much to change bonds of affection into bitter hatred. In such situations, it is best to break the family up and let everyone go his or her own way.

20 April 1996

Doing the dirty on women

I was hoping that the eleventh Lok Sabha
would have more women MPs than any of
the previous ten. Seeing the number of women
candidates put up by the major political parties
contesting the poll, it is pretty certain that
far from increasing their representation from
thirty-three in the tenth Lok Sabha, it will come
down to the lowest ever since Independence:
of every 100 candidates fighting the elections,
barely three are women, not all by any means
likely to win. It is clear that the next Lok Sabha
with over 540 members may have twenty less
women in it. If this is not discrimination, I do
not know what the word means.

It can be assumed that half the population
of our country is female. Going by numbers
alone, nearly half of the members of the
Lok Sabha should be women. That ideal
representation is never likely to be achieved; it
never has in any democratic legislative body.
The reason is simple: politics and social work
never have been, nor are ever likely to be high
priority with women. Women have to bear
most of the burdens of home-keeping, bearing

and rearing children, which do not leave them many options besides taking on part-time jobs: politics is a whole-time preoccupation.

Politics can be a very rough game; not many women can rough it out. Recall what Jayalalitha had to go through at M.G. Ramachandran's funeral, Laxmi Parvati, on the demise of N.T. Rama Rao, or what Mamata Banerjee had to face in Calcutta. There are not many women who will be willing to subject themselves to indignities even if the stakes are a chief ministership or membership of Parliament. As a result, a large number of women prefer to make a back-door entry into the political arena as widows, mistresses, daughters or daughters-in-law. Lots of male politicians also owe their entry into political life by being related to leaders: *kunbaprasthi* (nepotism) applies to both male and female relatives, but we have become used to sons, nephews and sons-in-law inheriting mantles of their elders, but not widows, mistresses, and daughters doing so.

Another handicap women suffer from is lack of lung power which is an essential requirement for mass leadership. Many women are good speakers but I can't think of one whom I would describe as a spellbinding orator. They can produce a Sushma Swaraj, a Margaret Alva and a few Uma Bharatis, but not any of the calibre of Atal Behari Vajpayee, Subhas Ghising, Bal Thakeray or Ajit Singh. Women's vocal chords are not designed to sway multitudes.

Having analyzed reasons for the paucity of women in public life, let me adduce reasons for having more of them in Vidhan Sabhas and the two houses of Parliament. They are better behaved and less prone to corruption than men. They know more about problems relating to their own sex and children. And once given positions of responsibility, they are more conscientious in discharging them. I am always reminded by the witty remark made by Charlotte Whitton, first lady to be elected Mayor of Ottawa: 'Whatever women do they must do twice as well as men to be thought half as good. Luckily, this is not difficult,' she said.

How do we ensure higher representation for women in our legislatures? Clearly not by appealing to leaders of different political parties to put up more women candidates for election.

All of them have been approached, all agreed to do so, but when it came to allocating tickets, none of them did. I do not think that passing legislation to ensure a third of the seats in legislative bodies for women is a very bright idea: In principle I am opposed to any kind of reservation on the basis of caste, religion, or gender. The only legitimate way of ensuring justice from political parties is for women's organizations and those who have been unfairly treated to serve an ultimatum to leaders of political parties, that unless they give women thirty-three per cent of the tickets, they will not get their votes.

Law courts versus hospitals

The two most depressing institutions one can visit in this country are hospitals and law courts: I feel less depressed visiting crematoriums and cemeteries. I have been fortunate in not having to go to a hospital as a patient—only to see friends and relatives undergoing treatment. In spite of pretty nurses whom one sees at times, I never want to change places with the patients. One can understand that since hospitals are full of sick people (and most big ones have morgues to keep corpses of those who die there), it would be silly to expect anything to be cheerful about them.

Law courts are another matter. In recent months I have had the misfortune of having to go to the courts many times. In no case was it of my own choice; every time I was there to defend myself. I had to waste many hours, many days waiting for my case to be heard, only to be told that the hearing had to be adjourned to another day, frequently to a distant date. But I got a feel of the atmosphere that pervades. Here were people in reasonably good physical shape but full of grievances against their kin, neighbours, landlords, tenants and others they think had wronged them. You could detect the tension in their faces as if their lives depended on whether they won or lost their cases. You don't see people smile or laugh in court except when a judge makes a witty remark (which they seldom do). Then there are lawyers rushing from one courtroom to the other as if their tails were on fire. I, for one, got the impression that law courts are not designed to dispense justice but to provide lawyers with a good livelihood. Most do pretty well for themselves: the toppers earning a comfortable Rs 1 lakh a day. Here too, there is a parallel with the medical profession: quite a few surgeons make as much as do the top lawyers. I am not very wrong in stating that a society in which lawyers and doctors flourish is a sick society—mentally sick to allow lawyers to live in clover; physically impaired, to allow doctors to thrive. So where would I prefer to be—in a court of law or a hospital? I can't make up my mind. But I do know that if I have to go on appearing in law courts much longer, I will soon have to be admitted to hospital.

Awakening

In recent months I have become a regular viewer of the Zee TV programme *'Jaagran'* (awakening). To start with, it has a lovely logo; the introductory song is equally apt:

Utth jaag musaafir bhore bhaee
Ab rayn kahan jo sovat hai
Jo sovat hai so khovat hai
Jo jagat hai so paawat hai

(Wayfarer arise! The sun has risen / The
night has fled / Why slumberest thou? /
Those who slumber are losers / Those
who are awake are gainers.)

So far I have heard six savants hold forth
on the need to better oneself: Murari Bapu,
Asaram Bapu, Singal, Goenka, Vaswani and
Satyananda. Of them, Singal and Vaswani
declaim in English; the others, in difficult
Hindi. Murari Bapu intersperses his sermons
with *bhajans* and chanting; so does Asaram
Bapu, but not as effectively. Besides, he has
a very irritating habit of whistling, and far
too often, ending his sentences with *'Jai Ram
ji ki bolna hoga.'* It is very similar to some
raagis who are in the habit of exhorting their
audiences to say *'Bolo Satnam Sri Wahguru!'*
These mannerisms diminish the solemnity of
what they are saying. However, my intention
is not to criticize what these good men have to

say about how we should look to God or the truth within ourselves; overcome lust, anger, greed, attachment and pride; nor do I carp about their recounting mythological tales and miracles which defy reason and logic because I learn much of what is popularly believed. What I would like to suggest in all humility to them is that seeing the enormous crowds that come to listen to their discourses, they should make their sermons more socially relevant to the needs of present-day society. None of them bother to do so. Why don't they talk about all-pervading corruption and exhort their followers to socially boycott those they know to be corrupt? Why don't they tell their admirers that they must not have large families in a country that is already overcrowded? Why don't they exhort their followers to plant trees and be kind to animals as a part of their religious duty? Religion which does not cater to the needs of the society is no religion; it is only a game of words.

27 April 1996

Beginning of a new era

Before leaving for Germany and Austria I had
expressed fears that by the time I returned home
a fortnight later, India would have changed
beyond recognition politically. I scanned all
the English papers I could in Hamburg, Berlin,
Vienna, Munich and Frankfurt, and saw my
dire prophecy being fulfilled. Right-wing
Hindu parties had done better than others; the
Congress, worse than it has ever done before;
the third force holding the balance of power.
The last Indian news I heard on TV before
leaving my Frankfurt hotel for the airport was
that Jyoti Basu was among the front runners
for the prime ministership of the country.
Although I had not forecast this, I had, in
an answer to a question put by a foreign
correspondent, said that though I could not
hazard any guesses about the man who would
become prime minister, the man I would like
to see replace P.V. Narasimha Rao was Jyoti
Basu. I am still of the same view. I am back
home in time for the horse-trading to begin.
How long will any government which is at the
mercy of its coalition partners, hope to last?

I have no regrets about Narasimha Rao. He proved to be a second-rate prime minister, and an unmitigated disaster for the Congress party. His reluctance to quit the post of party president and leader of the parliamentary party only went to show that he had less concern for the party and the country's future and more for himself. Calculated political cunning is not the same as leadership. What India needs today is a statesman dedicated to achieving certain goals for the people he leads. Rao was singularly lacking in these qualities.

There can be no doubt that the BJP has established its right to be the first to be called on to form the government. But at the moment it seems there is little chance of its getting sizeable support from smaller parties to gain a majority in Parliament. The President may soon have to call upon the commonly-chosen leader of other parties to form the next government. The mantle should have fallen on the shoulders of Jyoti Basu. Although over eighty, he is mentally and physically fit enough to discharge the duties of a prime minister. He has many other plus points. His record in office as chief minister of West Bengal for nineteen long years is untainted: no charges of corruption or nepotism (not even of favouring his own son Chandan Basu) have been levelled against him. Having a Marxist background, he has never descended to exploiting religious sentiment to gain popularity, never kow-towed to godmen or sought the advice of astrologers. This cannot be said about any other contenders for the top post. Above all, Jyoti Basu is better qualified to turn back the tide of Hindu fundamentalism represented by the BJP, VHP, Shiv Sena, Bajrang Dal and the RSS, than anyone else. The new prime minister must know that there are many more important things to be done than building a Ram mandir at Ayodhya. There is, for instance, the task of building the nation. Jyoti Basu is our best bet for heading an enlightened, forward-looking government. It is a thousand pities that his party has decided not to field him.

Now that Atal Behari Vajpayee has been sworn in as prime minister, I wish him well. He is a good, honest and able man, but in the wrong party. He has the charismatic qualities of Pandit Nehru, is a much better orator and poet, and could, if he won the confidence of the Muslims, Christians and other minorities which his coalition partners do not enjoy, make a truly great leader of the calibre that India deserves.

German yatra: Travel travails

They say travel broadens people's minds. If that is true, my mind should be as broad as the mighty Brahmaputra in flood. I have been just about everywhere in the world and seen all there is to see. I feel like a man who has been in a picture gallery one hour too long, and it is time to depart. My motto now is 'travel only if you must'. However, whenever an invitation from a foreign country comes my way, without thinking twice, I accept it. And as immediately, regret having done so. The first daunting problem is the business of getting visas: many forms to fill, photographs to attach, fees to pay and queuing up in front of visa counters to wait your turn to answer questions. All foreign embassies assume that you mean to flee your country and settle in theirs. You are made to feel utterly unwelcome. Many a time after I have got all my travel documents in hand, I remind myself of the times one had to do a lot more—small pox and yellow fever injections, income tax clearances and permits to go abroad. I look forward to the day when visas will be abolished and we will be treated like citizens of the world.

Another off-putting feature of going abroad is that all international flights from Delhi take off (and arrive) at unearthly hours between midnight and dawn. With having to report three hours before the flight time, one's night's sleep is lost. It's too late for dinner, too early for breakfast, and one is in no mood to watch the movies they put on for your entertainment.

The Indira Gandhi International Airport gets more crowded by the day. Other airports like the ones in Singapore and Bangkok are now much swankier than the airports in London, Paris or Frankfurt. Not Delhi. When many flights come in or leave about the same time, there is hardly any place to sit. For the first time I whiled away my time in Air India's Maharajah lounge. It is located alongside two more brightly lit and more frequented lounges. Our Maharajah lounge is as decadent as the tribe that bears its name. The atmosphere was funereal: dim lights, dilapidated sofas, nondescript paintings on the walls. I gulped down a glass of Pepsi cola (it would have been sacrilegious to taste good Scotch in the morgue) and went down to the general waiting room full of Japanese, French and Sardarjis. There was much more *raunaq* there than in the VIP lounge. And as if to brighten up the hall, the Indian cricket team led by Azharuddin and his boys came in trailed by autograph hunters. They were led past the queue to board their flight to London. No grievance: such privileges should be accorded to the nation's heroes. It only occurred to me that these young men who look so formidable on the TV screen are really like *chokras* still in college.

Air India does not have much of a reputation for punctuality. But my flight to Frankfurt left on the dot. I was dismayed to see that more than half the seats were empty. But the airline has prettier air hostesses than any other international airline. And they are ever so winsome and courteous.

I had a night of nine long hours ahead of me strapped in a chair with nothing to do except

eat, drink, watch films or listen to music.
Instead, I chose to watch the immense stretch
of darkness beneath me. Six hours later, the
darkness was frequently broken by the lights
of the cities over which we flew. I realized we
were over European air space. More reading
lights were switched on, queues began to form
outside the few lavatories, children began
to bawl for attention. Air hostesses looking
as fresh as ever hustled around with trays of
glasses of fruit juice and hot coffee. Breakfast
was served. Frankfurt was only an hour away.

I changed planes to get to Hamburg,
its largest sea port, the most important on
the Baltic Sea. The river Elbe flows through
the city. It is full of waterways and gardens.
I also recalled it as being a wicked city with
its notorious Reeperbahn lined with brothels
where middle-aged prostitutes eke out a living
from sailors and foreign tourists. This is
where I had seen my first live sex show. I also
recalled its unique form of greeting: one man
greets another with 'Humel Humel', the other
replies, 'Morse, Morse.' Humel, I am told, was
an ungainly water carrier who carried buckets
balanced on his shoulders. Street urchins would

pursue him calling out his name. He would reply in the local dialect with 'Morse, Morse' which means 'Kiss my bum'.

25 May 1996

New *netas*, new problems

For four days the entire nation was glued to their TV sets listening to debates on the two motions of confidence—one moved by the BJP and the other by the United Front coalition. Despite the rowdy behaviour of a large number of MPs, it has to be conceded that the standard of debate was higher than it has ever been in living memory. The star performers in support of the BJP were Atal Behari Vajpayee (a bit too histrionic, and addressing Hindu supporters outside the House), Jaswant Singh and Sushma Swaraj, supported by George Fernandes and Surjit Singh Barnala. From the other side there were splendid orations by Chidambaram, Pilot and, believe it or not, P.V. Narasimha Rao. There was much give and take on both sides. BJP and its supporters quite rightly focussed on the charges of corruption against ministers and civil servants during the Congress regime; the United Front focussed on the menace of Hindu fundamentalism sponsored by the Sangh Parivar. The debate clearly proved that the two problems uppermost in the minds of our legislators as well as the people are corruption and exploitation of religious sentiments for political gains. I am not sure which is the greater evil, but I do know, as does everyone else, that unless this two-headed monster is crushed once for all, we can say goodbye to stable governments and development.

The nation has run out of patience with corrupt politicians salting money away in foreign banks. Every morning we read of thousands of crores disappearing into the pockets of ministers and their relations. They are named by investigative agencies; FIRs are lodged against them, warrants of arrest issued, some go to jail, most get bail—and then we forget all about the affairs. Vajpayee was right when he said we do not care whether or not these felons are put behind bars, but we must get the money (our money) stashed away in foreign banks back into our country.

The debate also clearly showed the sharp division between the supporters of Hindutva and secular India—the two are not compatible. I sensed that the Sangh Parivar has realized that although exploiting the name of Sri Rama and breaking the mosque at Ayodhya may have won them the votes of illiterate, misguided Hindus, it has cost them the support of the educated and enlightened members of their community. It is not Hindu versus Muslim, Christian or Sikh but the backward-looking Hindu versus the forward-looking Hindu. If the Parivar hopes to come into power, it will have to do a lot of introspection and make radical changes in its political programme.

22 June 1996

Wife-bashing, Indian style

One evening, there was a lot of screaming, shouting of abuse and sounds of fisticuffs from the servants' quarters behind our block of apartments. We ran to see what was going on. A man was beating a woman with a stick

calling her a *randi* (whore) and *kaamchor*
(shirker) among other things. The woman was
screaming *'Hai hai bachao!'* (Save me). The
circle of men and women that had collected
round the couple were pleading *'Bas kaafee
ho gayaa; ab isse maaf kar do* (Stop, that's
enough; now forgive her). I burst in on the
scene, caught the fellow by the scruff of his
neck and shouted, *'Besharam! Aurat pe haath
utthatha hai!'* (Shameless creature, how dare
you raise your hand on a woman?)

The reaction of the man, the woman he
was beating, and the spectators, took me by
surprise. *'Meree aurat hai; tumhara kya lena
dena hai?'* (She is my wife; what business is it
of yours?) asked the man. The woman seemed
to acquiesce. So did the crowd. *'Sardarji, aap
is mein mat paro; ghareyloo jhagra hai, aap
niptaa leyngey'* (Sardarji, don't get involved in
this; it is a domestic quarrel, they'll resolve it
themselves).

I was made to feel like an interloper.
I found out that all the woman was guilty of
was having cooked a bad meal for her husband
who had returned home late and somewhat
drunk. It had happened before; she took the

chastisement as punishment she deserved. All said and done, she was his *gharwalee* (home-keeper), and if she failed him in any way, he had the right to punish her. I had no business interfering.

In India, being beaten is accepted as a hazard of being married. It is a common phenomenon among the peasantry and the poor. If a wife goes to a police station to lodge a complaint, in all probability the policemen, who also regularly beat their wives, will throw her out. She also gets no sympathy from her husband's family. On the contrary, her mother-in-law and sister-in-law thoroughly enjoy her discomfiture.

It would be an error to assume that wife-beating is confined to the illiterate and the poor. It is common enough among the educated and well-to-do. It is only when a woman is driven to desperation, or when in addition to beating his wife, a man consorts with other women, that the ill-treated wife will report her husband to the police, take her case to a woman's court, ask for separation or divorce. The odds are weighed heavily against her. Married men prone to sadism literally get away with murder.

I have no bright ideas of how to combat wife-bashing except that I do not accept it as a *'ghareyloo mamla'*. It should be a matter of concern for the entire society. Personally, I have a strong revulsion for men who abuse or beat their women. I cut such men out of my life because I regard wife-beating barbarous and unforgivable. Men who hit their women have no right to be admitted in civilized society. They should be expelled from all clubs, and people who feel as strongly on the subject as I do should share no *hookah-paanee* with them. Unless we can raise strong public opinion against wife-beaters, wife-beating will continue.

29 June 1996

How silly can we be?

Do you think that increasing the number of women members in the Lok Sabha and the Rajya Sabha from the present 20-40 to 130-140 will really better the lot of women in our country? Will it reduce the incidence of female foetus abortions? Will it reduce the numbers of female infanticide? Will it stop discrimination at home between boys and girls? Will it lessen demands for dowry, maltreatment of daughters-in-law, wife-bashing, deaths in contrived accidents and neglect of widows? The answer to everyone of these questions will be no, no, no, no. Then why this silly exercise to amend the Constitution and ensure that in the future, a third of our MPs should be women?

The answer is simple: It is a cheap way of earning credit as a champion of women's rights in the hope of getting their votes. If the amendment proposed is passed, you can be sure about who will reap its benefits. Take a look at the sitting lady MPs, MLAs and ladies who contest elections: a sizeable proportion are wives, daughters, daughters-in-law, and at times mistresses, of politicians in power. Their numbers will multiply. To the rest of the world we will have a window display of more women legislators than any other country of the world; behind the facade, there will be very little to show in the way of having improved the wretched lot of our women. Take a look at the number of women in the British House of Commons, the French, German, Italian or Spanish parliaments, the US Congress or the Senate. They are less than one-tenth the number of men. And yet, the lot of their women is a hundred times better than that of ours. Our women have the same rights as the men to vote and stand for elections. If they want to become MLAs or MPs, let them do so in the same way as their men folk—without wanting reservation of seats.

If we really want to raise our women from their present lowly status to equality with men, we have to provide them free education up to the highest levels, subsidize their feeding, clothing and accommodation. Thereafter, let them fend for themselves and show that what men can do, women can do better.

21 September 1996

Old age and leadership

A sizeable proportion of the American population is of the opinion that Bob Dole at seventy-two is too old to be President of the

United States. The average American in his seventies is a lot fitter physically and mentally than the average Indian in his sixties. On TV you can see sprightly Americans of Bob Dole's age group going up and down the steps of an aircraft or jump up to podiums to make speeches. Then compare them to those of our leaders who are younger than them. Notice President Shankar Dayal's ungainly, duck-like waddle as he walks to the microphone; his mind may be as sharp as ever but he is evidently not as fit as he should be. Our ex-prime minister, Narasimha Rao (75), has had heart bypass surgery; so has Sitaram Kesri (80) who has taken over as president of the Congress. He may be a shrewd and honest politician but does he have the physical energy to revitalize a party which seems to be afflicted with terminal cancer?

There are other instances of physical lethargy amongst our leaders. Our new prime minister, though he claims to come from robust rustic stock, is evidently finding desk work too much for his constitution. His chronic irritability, particularly when facing the media, confirms this suspicion. More than once he has

been photographed yawning with his mouth
wide open or in deep slumber at public meetings.
Atal Behari Vajpayee, so alert and lively as a
debater, is known to nod off while presiding
at meetings when others are speaking. It's not
boredom, it is physical fatigue. The only senior
Indian leader who is an exception to the rule
of ageing debility and who is all there in body
and mind, is the octogenarian chief minister of
West Bengal, Jyoti Basu.

It is time younger politicians took over
command of their respective parties. There
are many waiting in the wings: Chidambaram,
Sharad Pawar, Laloo Prasad Yadav, Madhavrao
Scindia, Mamata Banerji, Margaret Alva, Girija
Vyas, Renuka Chaudhuri, Vasundhara Raje,
Jayanti Natarajan, Pramod Mahajan, Sushma
Swaraj, Rajesh Pilot, Bansal, Bitta, Ambika
Soni and others in their forties and early fifties.

The concept of ageing has undergone
dramatic change since the days of Shakespeare.
For the bard it meant 'mere oblivion, sans
teeth, sans eyes, sans taste, sans everything'.
He was wrong in holding 'when age is in, wit
is out'. Today we have the phenomenon of the
'robust elderly' which makes seventy-two-year-

old Bob Dole almost a spring chicken. While his own countryman Mark Twain would have disqualified anyone who had crossed the scriptural statute of 'three score years and ten', a majority holds that age brings wisdom. And wisdom is what we expect from our leaders. There is no reason why we cannot combine the wisdom of elder statesmen with the youthful vigour of the younger generation.

5 October 1996

Bapu Gandhi's legacy

My favourite story about the Gandhian legacy that I concocted during the Emergency goes somewhat as follows: Bapu in heaven was much perturbed that few people in India even remembered his name. He sent for Pandit Nehru and asked him, 'You were prime minister of India for many years. What did you do to perpetuate my memory?'

Panditji replied: 'I did the best I could. I made a *samadhi* where we cremated you. On your birth and death anniversaries, we assemble there and sing your favourite hymns: *"Vaishnav jan to tainey kahiye jo peerh paraayee jaaney ray* and *Ishwar-Allah terey naam, sabko sanmatee dey Bhagwaan"*. So I ensured that at least twice a year we recall your memory.'

Bapu then sent for Lal Bahadur Shastri and put to him the same question. Shastri replied: 'Bapu, I was prime minister for only a very short time. I had your writings and speeches translated into all Indian languages and widely distributed. I had your statues put in prominent places in all cities, towns and villages. I had your birthday declared a public holiday. What more could I do in the time I had?'

Bapu then sent for Indira Gandhi who was ruling the country and asked her the same question. She replied, 'Bapu, I've done more than Shastri or my father to make your name immortal. I've made all your countrymen like you. I've left them with nothing but a *langotee* to cover their nakedness and a *danda* to help them to walk.'

Bapu was horrified. 'This is wrong. You will bring a rebellion on your head,' he protested.

'I've taken good care of that eventuality,' replied the over-confident Indira Gandhi. 'I have put the *langotee* round their necks and shoved the *danda* up their bottoms.'

On the last Gandhi Jayanti, I pondered over what the successors of our first three prime ministers would have said in answer to Bapu's questions—Morarji Desai, Charan Singh, Chandra Shekhar, Rajiv Gandhi, Narasimha Rao, Atal Behari Vajpayee and the present prime minister, Deve Gowda. Apart from the sanctimonious Morarji Desai who was at least truthful, the rest destroyed the Gandhian legacy with methodical unconcern for Gandhian values. Truthfulness gave way to trickery and lying; simple living to opulence; merit to nepotism. The truth of the adage *Jatha raja tatha praja*—as the ruler, so his subjects—was proved with a vengeance. Corruption seeped down from top to bottom. We became a corrupt nation. The one thing that Narasimha Rao did to fulfil Gandhi's wishes but not in the way that Bapu wanted, was to destroy the Indian National Congress. Another thing that Hindu fundamentalist parties, Bhajpa, VHP, Shiv Sena, the RSS and monkeys of the Bajrang Dal are hoping to achieve is to subvert Bapu's ideal of *Serva dharma samabhava* (equal respect for all religions) by trying to turn secular India into a Hindu Rashtra. It would be best to give up the humbug of celebrating Gandhi Jayantis.

In defence of Husain

I am truly pained to see the beginning of a wave of persecutions against our most revered painter Maqbool Fida Husain. I have seen almost everything he has painted: from horses, bulls, cows, Ganpatis, Hindu goddesses, Bajrang Bali, Indira Gandhi and Mother Teresa to the lovely Madhuri Dixit. I have detected nothing obscene in any of them. Naked, yes; obscene, no. But then we have so many naked representations of our gods and goddesses in paintings and temple sculptures. Nobody has said anything against them. You can see vivid portrayals of Parvati, Durga and Kali in copulation (Maithuna) with Lord Shiva; also pictures of Radha and Krishna in amorous intercourse in Pahari and Rajasthani paintings. Has anyone sought to have them burnt or destroyed? And what nonsense it is to accuse Husain of hurting the feelings of the Hindus! Are you picking on Husain because he is Muslim? It is time men like Pramod Nawalkar and Digvijay Singh (when did he last visit Khajuraho?) grew up and stopped pandering to the susceptibilities of the stupid masses. Husain is a great painter who has brought credit to his country. His works can be seen in art galleries and private collections all over the world.

19 October 1996

Maligning the Mahatma

Bal Thackeray is by no means the first and the only person to use abusive language for Mahatma Gandhi. Many of Gandhi's contemporaries, Indian and English, accused him of being devious, self-righteous, cunning and downright dishonest. His detractors were silenced by the exemplary courage he showed in his last days by bringing communal violence to an end in Calcutta, Noakhali and Delhi virtually single-handedly and paying the price for doing so by laying down his own life. One prayed and hoped that his critics had been silenced for ever. Alas!

Let us examine what some of his detractors had to say about him, and if there was any substance in what they said. There was, of course, Winston Churchill who called him the wily naked fakir. He can be forgiven because he did not know the man. Less known is what Lord Wavell, who was the viceroy of India (1943-47) before Lord Mountbatten, had to say. Though he concealed his hatred for Gandhi in public, his revulsion for him is expressed in his personal diary which has been published. In an entry dated September 26, 1946, he wrote: 'Gandhi at the end exposed Congress policy of domination more nakedly than ever before. The more I see of that old man, the more I regard him as an unscrupulous and old hypocrite; he would shrink from nonviolence and blood-letting to achieve his ends, though he would naturally prefer to do so by chicanery and a false show of mildness and friendship . . . His one idea for forty years has been to overthrow British rule and influence, and to establish a Hindu Raj; and he is unscrupulous as he is persistent.'

If Wavell had used the words 'Hindustani Raj' instead of 'Hindu Raj', I would have forgiven him as well.

Wavell's favourite epithets for Gandhi were 'malignant' and 'malevolent'. He continued: 'He is an exceedingly shrewd, obstinate, single-minded politician; and there is little true saintliness in him.'

Once again, Wavell could be pardoned because he was an imperialist who was convinced that British rule was the best thing that had ever happened to India and could not understand why any Indian would want to get rid of the British. But it is difficult to understand Indians criticizing the greatest son of India of our times. They have tried to damage his statues; they have tried to make his private life appear scandalous (as Bal Thackeray has done), and they have vilified him. Those of us who still believe in him have kept silent in the conviction that this is what he would have liked us to do. However, on the anniversary of his assassination, let us reaffirm our faith in our

Bapu. And let us assure the Bal Thackerays of this world that abusing Gandhi is like spitting at the sky; their spit will only fall on their faces.

18 January 1997

Republic Day 1997

My days of getting up in the early hours of a winter morning to occupy my seat in time to watch the Republic Day parade are long gone. For the past ten years I've watched the parade on TV. It's much the same thing year after year and my enthusiasm has declined with age. Also, I am not sure if we have very much to celebrate about. I won't go as far back as fifty years since we became independent to make a balance sheet of our achievements and failures, but only to the last twelve to draw your attention to the major trends which are shaping our nation. Three stand out on the debit side: increase in violence, corruption, and religious intolerance. And only one on the credit side: liberalization of economy leading to marginal decrease in poverty.

In 1984 Mrs Gandhi was murdered. Thousands of innocent Sikhs paid with their lives for the crime committed by two members of their community. Then came the assassination of Rajiv Gandhi in May 1991, followed a few months later by the destruction of the Babri Masjid and violence against Muslims wherever they protested against this form of medieval vandalism. Much of this violence was the outcome of politicians plotting to gain votes by playing one community against the other. Inevitably there was resurgence of religious intolerance. A perfectly valid judgement by the Supreme Court granting maintenance to Shah Bano was cast aside by an Act of Parliament to appease Muslim bigots. Religious fanaticism took its toll with the murder of, amongst others, Safdar Hashmi (January 1989), and last year, in the destruction of the paintings of M.F. Husain.

The single most sinister development of the past decade was the steep rise in corruption in high places involving a former prime minister, many ministers of his cabinet, chief ministers and senior bureaucrats. With the executive paralyzed by inaction and the legislature by wranglings of factions, came the increase in the role of the judiciary. The Supreme Court led by judges like Kuldip Singh and Varma pronounced judgements on matters which should normally have been the concern of the administration viz. forcing men in power to vacate houses which they had no right to occupy, preserving the environment, and protecting ancient monuments.

The one redeeming feature of Narasimha Rao's tenure as prime minister was his support of Manmohan Singh's liberalization of the economy, and giving free rein to private enterprise. It yielded handsome dividends and earned credit for the country and the finance minister who won acclaim for his ability and integrity. How many trends of the recent past will continue in the years to come is beyond my comprehension.

25 January 1997

Shobha De and gender wars

Shobha De has had the best of everything any Indian woman would wish for in her life. Daughter of a commissioner of police, ravishingly beautiful, two rich husbands with a French diplomat sandwiched between them, editor of three journals, author of eight books, every one of them making the bestseller list at the time of its publication. And now living in considerable splendour in a large apartment in Bombay with her second husband and six children—his, hers and theirs.

She is not the kind of sourpuss you would think of spewing venom in a long, bitchy thesis on why all men are bad. But this is precisely what she has done in her latest book *Surviving Men: The Smart Woman's Guide to Staying on Top*. It is the first non-fiction book she has written, but it also promises to become another bestseller because its theme, like the themes of her novels, is sex, with obscene four-letter words strewn liberally across every page. She also makes the most outrageous statements on male chauvinism that I have read. I would have dismissed it as frothy rubbish. I cannot because it is also irritatingly thought-provoking and highly readable.

Let us examine some of De's assertions: 'Sex appeal lies in the wallet of her beholder,' she writes. There may be some truth in that. We have always been told that money makes the mare go. But it applies equally to men and women. If a fat, rich man is more attractive to a woman than a handsome pauper, so is a matron loaded with diamonds more attractive to a man than a pretty Cinderella in tattered rags.

De goes on to assert that men should pay more attention to their teeth and oral hygiene—bad breath kills romance. 'Couples who floss together stay together,' she writes. I go along with that.

She may be right about men being unsure of their potency in middle age. But so are women beset with fears of losing their looks after menopause. Are men more mean than women? Or have less feelings than them? De thinks so. According to her, men have as much feelings as dogs or earthworms. What draws them towards women is their smell—not the perfume they wear but their body odour which is like Chinese sweet-and-sour dishes. What men like about women is not their looks but their availability. The more willing a woman, the more men are drawn to her like flies to a pot of honey.

'Most men are unfaithful to their wives or mistresses,' she asserts. They will play according to the rules of marriage 'till they discover the unadulterated joys of adultery'. How then can women love men? It is easier to love dogs and even plants. Men in love are tiresome. Another myth she seeks to explode is that 'couples who sleep together, stay together'. She advises separate bedrooms, bathrooms and vacations.

De maintains that there is no such thing as a platonic relationship between men and women. 'The only person ever to believe in platonic friendship was Plato.' Money and more than money, power makes men irresistible to women. Rajiv Gandhi, despite his good looks and power, did not pass De's test, as he was 'a softie with spaniel's eyes'. To evoke women's admiration, a leader has to inspire fear. Gandhi failed to do that and hence lacked sex appeal. Jinnah, because he was stern, aroused women much more. Clinton passes De's test with flying colours as he has good looks and power which he uses to bash up his adversaries.

All men are of course, mother-fixated. De advises women never to take on their mothers-in-law. They will always lose the battle.

However, she grudgingly concedes that women need men. She advises her sisters to treat them like donkeys, with carrots and sticks. All they want is food, booze and sex—in that order. When he becomes too obstinate, say 'no' and he will come round begging with his tail between his legs.

That is Shobha De for you. You can't do without her. You have to read whatever she writes.

8 February 1997

Authors and publishers

A lively, at times acerbic exchange of views on the relationship between authors and their publishers has been going on between Ashok Chopra of the UBSPD on the one side, D.N. Malhotra (Hind Pocket Books) and Narendra Kumar (Har Anand) on the other. All three are publishers. I am constrained to enter the fray as I am both an author and closely connected with three publishing houses, Penguin India, Orient Longman and my son-in-law's own,

Ravi Dayal Publisher. I have not the slightest doubt that Ashok Chopra is right in saying that many Indian publishers do not give their authors either money owed to them in royalties nor the respect due to them as people who make publishing a profitable business.

Readers may not know that authors are rarely entitled to more than twelve per cent of the price of their books. Usually it is between five to ten per cent. Many publishers do not pay a single paisa of what is due to their authors. They do not render accounts of their earnings and think that authors should be content to see their names in print. There are quite a few of this tribe who instead of paying authors royalties, actually charge them the costs of printing in advance, and make them buy copies of their own books. Some render false accounts and compel authors to buy unsold stocks. If provoked, I will gladly furnish names of these publishing houses to publishers' organizations. I will not do so in the press lest I be involved in tiresome litigation. All I will request publishers to do is to examine their own consciences and ask themselves if they are being fair to their authors. I do not consider people who pay for the publication of their books merely to give them away as presents to their friends as being authors in the proper sense of the term. An author is one who lives on his writing. To deprive him of his dues is robbery.

My friend Arun Shourie has found a way to circumvent publishers. He has his books printed and bound himself. A distributor lifts his entire stock. Arun earns sixty per cent in royalties in one transaction. I, and authors like me pray that we get our meagre royalties spread over the years in time. We who generate books get the smallest share of the lolly. Publishers, distributors and bookstore owners divide the rest of the loot between them. Is this fair?

15 February 1997

There is more to life

I should be writing about the budget session of Parliament, about politicians and about corruption cases in the courts. But like the rest of you, I am bored stiff reading about them day after day for weeks on end. There is more to life than the doings of crooks and criminals. It is much better to turn one's gaze away from these things. There are, for instance, changes in seasons and renewal of life. It is springtime, and with spring, hope of better things to come.

Come *Basant Panchami*, and the winter's cold loses its sting. The *paalaa* (cold) is really *urant* (flown away). How much closer our *desi* calendar is to the changes of seasons than the Roman calendar: *Sarson* (mustard) flowers have withered; the mulberry tree outside my window is in new leaf; *kachnars* (bauhenias) have sprouted snow-white and pink blossoms. In another few days, the *tesu* (flame of the forest) will usher in Holi. The all-too-short spring will give way to the all-too-long summer months.

Songs of new life can be seen everywhere. Cock sparrows fluff out their wings and hop around the hens with lustful chirpings. Crows can be seen on the lawns tempting possible mates by presenting them with twigs to make nests. Koels keep a watchful eye on the crows' possible nesting sites where they can deposit their eggs and have a good time while the crows are cuckolded into nursing their young.

Barbets call from dawn to dusk. The *papeeha* (Brainfever bird) announces the onset of hot days with *Paos-ala! Paos-ala!* (summer is coming) also rendered as *Pee kahaan? Pee kahaan?* (Where is my beloved?)

With so much that is beautiful going on around us, do we have to ruin our moods and appetite by dwelling on dung heaps piled up by dirty politicians? Let them squabble and make more money. Let them go to hell.

8 March 1997

It will not work

By now our rulers should have learnt three things from experience: one, that enacting laws which cannot be enforced will expose the law-embracing agencies like the police and the judiciary to ridicule and temptation; two, that banning something is the surest way of increasing its demand and encouraging people to devise ways to get round the law. And finally, there are things that are better done by persuasion than by force. The best examples are attempts at prohibiting drinking and smoking. Prohibition has proved to be an expensive flop wherever it has been tried. Alcohol has always been easily available in prohibition states like Gujarat, Andhra Pradesh and Tamil Nadu. At the moment, it is risky drinking in Haryana, but within a few months after the administrative enthusiasm to impose prohibition has cooled, it will go the same way as Gujarat and Tamil Nadu. As for the ban on smoking in public places, I cannot think of anything sillier than the Delhi Government trying to enforce it. Do these fellows apply their minds to problems before coming out with foolish answers? Have they nothing better to do than interfere with people's personal lives?

Mr Chandrababu Naidu of Andhra Pradesh has realized the folly of enforcing prohibition and has been wise enough to modify the law by maintaining a ban on spurious hooch and arrack but allowing wholesome liquor to be sold openly. The enormous loss the state suffered through the loss of excise revenue and futile attempts to enforce prohibition will be made up by the reopening of breweries, vineries and distilleries. Chaudhari Bansi Lal of

Haryana should learn from the experience of Andhra Pradesh. Like the late N.T. Rama Rao, Mr Bansi Lal cashed in on the votes of battered wives and deprived families of irresponsible drunkards, but like Mr Chandrababu Naidu, he will understand that he cannot offload his state's debts on the centre. By all means teach people that alcohol, drugs and tobacco taken in excess are injurious to health and the well-being of one's family; by all means send do-gooders like Swami Agnivesh to preach against the evils of drinking, but a blanket ban on alcohol will not work. That is quite clear and plain, simple commonsense.

5 April 1997

National Natak Mandali

I have come to the conclusion that our politicians are better actors than our film stars. They do not need scriptwriters to tell them what to say, they do not need directors to tell them how to say what they have to say; they can lie with such straight faces, that we who watch them on TV or read their statements in newspapers believe every word they utter. It takes us a long time to realize that they take us for a ride by lying to us all the time. Unfortunately no democracy can function without politicians. So we have to resign ourselves to our fate and hope that some miracle will throw up a new breed of political leaders dedicated more to their country than to themselves, and that lying to the people amounts to letting down the people.

This brings me to the likelihood of change of government at the Centre. Whether or not the United Front Government is or is not voted out of power (at the time of writing this piece I have no idea), I am convinced that the *khichdi* of the thirteen parties that form the United Front has outlived its utility: if it survives this challenge it will only get a breather and fall a few months later. Though it has a few capable ministers, Deve Gowda has failed to inspire confidence in the people. His hobnobbing with religious fundamentalists and fascists has unmasked his pretension to secularism. He is not prime minister material.

Is Sitaram Kesri prime minister material? I cannot vouch for him except that while in control of vast sums of money for the Congress party over many long years, he did not feather his nest, acquired no property for himself or let any of his close relatives or friends amass wealth. His credentials as a secularist are also impeccable. He is free of the taint of communal prejudice and more acceptable to the religious minorities than any other Hindu leader. I do not know much about his administrative capabilities but he can muster up a team more dynamic and honest than any that Narasimha Rao had or Deve Gowda has.

Murdering one's ancestors

There was a time when I spent my winter weekends exploring old monuments extending from Hauz Khas to Suraj Kund. I spent many nights in the Qutub dak bungalow and wandered round the Mehrauli complex of ancient ruins extending from the Shamsi Talab, Auliya Masjid and Jahaz Mahal down to the mansions of the Omarah and the tomb of Jamali-Kamali. I discovered many old *baolis* (stepwells). But the one thing I was looking for was Balban's grave, which I never found.

Twenty years ago you could go from Safdarjang to Mehrauli, from the Qutub Minar to Tuglaqabad and Suraj Kund and get one uninterrupted view of the ruins of ancient monuments of pre-Mughal days. They made a spectacular sight. Today, you can't see any of them because housing colonies have come up around them and the monuments themselves are occupied by squatters. In mosque courtyards buffaloes are tethered, mausoleum walls are marked as wickets for boys playing cricket; where the sultans of Delhi held court, *chaiwalas* ply their trade. Tiny Jat and Gujjar habitations that had grown up around these monuments have been swallowed up by New Delhi's insatiable appetite for expansion.

Seventy years ago I used to cycle from Jantar Mantar Road where we lived, to Modern School, then in Daryaganj. The part of the journey I looked forward to most was riding along a road from Ajmeri Gate, past Turkman Gate to Delhi Darwaza, enter the walled city to reach my school at the city's eastern end. It was memorable because I rode along the Mughal wall stretching uninterrupted for over a mile. The wall no longer exists: instead we have the noisy, ugly Asaf Ali Road, without character or history.

It is hard to believe that these acts of vandalism of our historic city took place in the regimes of our two most forward-looking prime ministers, Jawaharlal Nehru and Indira Gandhi. The Mughal wall was pulled down in the name of slum clearance in Nehru's time with Nehru's approval. No one was consulted and no opinions sought. The smothering of monuments of the Sultanate period took place during Indira Gandhi's rule. This killing by strangulation could and should have been avoided if provision had been made for parks round the monuments and no one allowed to misuse them as homes or for commerce.

12 April 1997

The debate

On April 11, I refused to have any engagements. I wanted to listen to the debate on the United

Front's motion seeking a vote of confidence on its performance. I was so eager not to miss a single word that I switched on my TV set twenty minutes ahead of time. Doordarshan was showing a film on monkeys: rhesus langurs, chimpanzees, gorillas and a *bandarwala* persuading his reluctant monkey named Hira Lai to marry a pretty *bandaree*. After many a whisper into their ears, the couple agreed to be united in matrimony. Monkeys were followed by a short programme for children. A lady teacher was telling her class about the habits of crocodiles. She had a cloth model of the reptile with its mouth wide open displaying rows of sharp teeth with which it could *harrup* fish and smaller animals. I am not sure if Doordarshan intended to prepare viewers for what was to come, or whether it was mere coincidence.

I am being unfair to our legislators: like others I am disenchanted with their performance. Contrary to my expectation, there was a lot of fiery oratory. That was to be expected when everyone was eager to project himself as a true patriot above communal prejudices. The treasury benches could have been more eloquent about the government's performance. I did not expect any fireworks from Deve Gowda, but I.K. Gujral who has solid achievements to his credit was strangely subdued and colourless. Jaswant Singh of the BJP was at his sarcastic best and set the tone of the debate. He asked what made the Congress president Sitaram Kesri choose March 30 to drop his bombshell: The prime minister was in Moscow, Mr Nelson Mandela in Delhi, Indo-Pak talks were going on, the NAM conference was due, the Sheikh of Oman was on a state visit and, above all, the budget was yet to be passed. No MP has answers to these questions. The threat of dissolution of the Lok Sabha and the fear of going back to the polls hung like the sword of Damocles over their heads.

It was the first time I heard Pramod Mahajan. Despite my detestation of BJP's communal approach to national problems, I was compelled to concede that I had not heard such powerful oratory in Parliament. Much of Mahajan's fire was doused by Chidambaram's well-reasoned and well-worded speech. No rhetoric but cold logic in favour of the prime necessity of commitment to secular ideals. And needless to say, Vajpayee once again proved that.when it comes to speechifying he remains numero uno. So charged was the atmosphere that even Deve Gowda's swansong was more coherent than any of his speeches over the ten months he was prime minister.

There were many good speeches by leaders like Indrajit Gupta, Somnath Chatterjee, Priyaranjan Das Munshi, Nitish Kumar, Barnala and others. I was left wondering why men so gifted in oratory were so poor in governance.

19 April 1997

Faith and fanaticism

The worst enemy of every religion is the fanatic who professes to follow it and tries to impose views of his faith on others. All religions have had and have today, bigots who give founders of their religion and their teachings a bad name. People do not judge religion by what their prophets were like or what they preached but by the way the followers of their religion practice it. Christians had their inquisitors who burnt innocent men and women at the stake as heretics. Muslims have their Islamic fraternities whose leaders pronounce fatwas condemning people to death; ordering women to shroud themselves in veils, and imposing draconian rules of behaviour on the community. Sikhs had their Bhindranwale who forbade men to dye or roll up their beards, women to wear saris or jeans, put bindis on their foreheads, and said nasty things about *dhotian-topian waaley*— those who wear dhotis and caps (the Hindus). At one time the presence of a Sikh in a bus or a rail compartment inspired confidence among the passengers; today, thanks to Bhindranwale's legacy, the presence of a Sikh creates nervousness among non-Sikhs. Not to be outdone, Hindus produced their own fanatics who condemn Christianity and Islam as alien religions, and while mouthing platitudes about being the most tolerant religion on earth, hound Christian missionaries and target Muslim places of worship for destruction. In the name of Shri Ram, they demolished the Babri Masjid in Ayodhya.

Of all the world's religions, the most misunderstood and maligned is Islam. Since it challenged Christian hegemony over other religions, Christians were disposed to find fault with everything it stood for and resurgent Muslim fundamentalism gave them all the ammunition they needed to castigate it. Retrograde laws imposing purdah on women, interpreting the *Shariah* in a manner that implies murderers should be beheaded and women caught in adultery should be maimed and stoned to death. Today Islam is judged not by the teachings of the *Koran* or the sayings of Prophet Mohammed but by the doings of the Taliban in Afghanistan and Muslim fundamentalists in other countries.

At the same time, there are good people and good scholars in all religious communities who wage a losing battle in trying to inform people of the true nature of their faiths.

Unfortunately, whatever they tell us about true Islam, Muslims will continue to be judged by the acts of groups like the Taliban and the Mujahideens who wage unending wars against the non-Muslims—in the same way that Hinduism will be judged by the utterances of women like Uma Bharati and Sadhvi Rithambara and the doings of

Bal Thackeray's Shiv Sainiks, Vishwa Hindu Parishad and Bajrang Dal followers. It is a great pity that fanaticism always wins the battle against true faith.

24 May 1997

A Sphinx called Sonia

The Sphinx is said to have an inscrutable smile: nobody knows what amuses her in the solitary desert wastes where she has sat for centuries staring vacantly into space. The same applies to our Sonia Gandhi. We all know she is the widow of the handsome prime minister who, though not very bright, was much loved as an Indian Prince Charming. Sonia has quite a few things in common with her late husband. She too is an extremely attractive person and shares her husband's loathing for politics and politicians. People who loved her husband have invested her with the aura he had. Her refusal to be drawn into the dirty game of party politics has enhanced people's respect for her. No one regarded her as a member of the Congress party—everyone thought of her as the unofficial 'Rajmata' and the rightful representative of the Nehru-Gandhi family.

Sonia Gandhi has plenty to keep her busy: she is chairperson of several organizations connected to her late husband and his family. It is her involvement in these non-political activities which earned her respect and affection which cut across party lines. This brings into question the wisdom of her enrolling herself as a primary member of the Congress party. It transforms her into a political figure and as such, not acceptable to those who do not approve of the Congress party's political programmes. She has done herself disservice. Those who pressurized her into joining the party (primarily Sitaram Kesri) have not only harmed her image but also the country by depriving it of a figure hitherto regarded as above politics and someone the people could turn to for unbiased service.

Attempts are afoot to persuade Sonia Gandhi to become President of the Congress. She will be well advised not to fall into the trap. For one, she is not qualified to hold the exalted post; for another, those behind the move are both dishonest and foolish. They are dishonest because their only motive is to exploit the affection people have for Sonia for their own, their political and the party's gains at the next general election. They are foolish because they think that her becoming President will make a great difference to the party's fortunes. It will not. She will certainly be able to win the traditional family seat from Amethi or Rae Bareli. But no more. And once she becomes politically active, the Opposition will tear her reputation to shreds. Her association with Quattrocchi and her husband's connection with the Bofors deal will be played up in order to plague her. In her own interests it would be best if she kept her distance from all politicians. A silent Sonia with the enigmatic smile of the Sphinx while keeping everyone guessing, will ensure her longevity as the nation's Rajmata.

14 June 1997

Fair deal for women

It would be unfair to assume that those against thirty-three per cent reservation of seats in legislatures for women are anti-women. Far from it. I would like to see half the seats in the legislatures occupied by women. But not by an Act of Parliament. Many of us including women feel that reserving seats for any community or a section of society is bad in principle and does not make the slightest impact on the lot of common men or women. We abolished separate electorates and reservation of seats for religious minorities (Muslims, Christians and Sikhs). The number of Muslims and Christians in state legislatures and the Lok Sabha declined rapidly for the simple reason that these two communities are scattered all over the country and only in a couple of districts are in majority to ensure their being elected. Our people still like to vote for members of their own community. Political parties like to give tickets to candidates who are likely to win. So both Muslims and Christians are grossly under-represented in elective bodies. The Sikhs manage to hold their own because they are largely concentrated in one region (Punjab) and do send more members to the Legislative Assembly and the Lok Sabha than their under two per cent of the population would warrant. Should we reintroduce reservation of seats for Muslims and Christians as we have done for Scheduled Castes and other backward communities? Have these reservation of seats improved the lot of these deprived communities? They have not. Only the well-to-do among them have been able to avail of this special privilege. It will be the same if we grant women thirty-three per cent representation by law.

Will having a third of every elective body improve the lot of poor Indian women? Will men stop ill-treating their wives? Will fathers of daughters not have to cough up dowries beyond their means to find them husbands? Will husbands and in-laws stop torturing girls who come into their families as brides, for not bringing larger dowries with them? Will bride-burning and bride suicides decline? None of these things will happen overnight.

I agree that women must have more representation in Vidhan Sabhas and Parliament. But the onus for doing so must be on the political parties—they should field more women in elections, see that they win rather than take refuge in an Act of Parliament that abrogates their own responsibility.

Don't change my TV channel

For one who for years boasted that he did not
have a TV set, it is hard to admit that now he
cannot do without it. I am far from being a
couch potato, but I do spend quite some time
watching news broadcasts by four channels:
Doordarshan, Star TV, BBC and CNN and
sometimes a fifth one, Pak TV. Of the news
channels, my top favourite is Star TV. I watch
cricket, tennis and hockey matches on whatever
channels they are available. On Sundays,
I watch both the *adalats* (Rajat Sharma's on
Star TV and Raghuvansh's on Zee). Music is
another of my passions: classical Hindustani,
Carnatic and lighter stuff. What I enjoy most
is *'Antakshari'* on Zee TV. I also love watching
nature programmes, and when my cable
operator deprives me of the Discovery channel,
I ring him up and scream blue murder till it is
restored.

I also watch certain programmes because
they are unbelievably bad. On the top of my
hate list are *bhajans* sung in praise of Santoshi
Mata, *Sheyran Walleye* (Goddess Durga),
Hey Bholeynath and a few others of the kind.

They are unethical, badly produced and utterly mindless. Far from inculcating a scientific temper, they preach superstition and belief in the occult. *Parvachans* broadcast in *'Jagran'* come a close second on my hate list. I watch them only to be able to write with authority that I think they could be a lot better if they preached good behaviour towards one's fellow human beings instead of narrating tales from the epics or telling people that the ultimate ambition of every human being should be to place his head on the lotus feet of a guru.

Who am I to tell people what they should watch and enjoy? Each one to his taste. As long as we have the right to choose what we want to see, we have no right to grumble. That is why I am alarmed with the provisions of the Broadcasting Bill which is to be presented to Parliament. If passed, it will severely limit the choice of cable channels available to us. Most of the best are foreign-based. We do not have, nor will have, the means of producing programmes of the calibre of Discovery or Star TV. There is little justification for meddling with the present arrangement. Doordarshan enjoys a near monopoly viewership (over eighty-five per cent). Of the fifty-four million homes that have TV, satellite channels are viewed by a mere fourteen million. In no democratic countries are such restrictions imposed on foreign programmes as are envisaged in our Broadcasting Bill. Our government proposes to set up a Broadcasting Authority which will include non-officials. Past experience shows that as soon as the government sets up a supervisory body and introduces licences, it leads to meddling and corruption. There is already a Cable Network Regulation Act of 1994. It has done nothing to improve the quality of films shown on TV. Supporters of the bill in question talk about the dangers of a cultural invasion. This is absolute rubbish. If there is any danger of our culture being swamped, it is not from the outside but by the rot that has set inside. Take a second look at the wretched song and jerky hip movements of the most popular songs and the inane depictions of our gods and goddesses and ask yourself, 'Is this Indian culture?'

21 June 1997

VIP as Nuisance Number One

Photographs showed the prime minister, chief minister of Delhi, health minister of the Central Government, health minister of the state and the Lieutenant-Governor of Delhi all in one room enquiring about the well-being of one of the victims of the Uphaar cinema fire tragedy. None of these worthies even knew the name of the man whose well-being had brought them to his hospital bedside. However, the head of the AIIMS (where many of the injured were brought), brazenly stated that VIP visits did not affect the smooth working of the institute. He was of course, talking through his hat. If he had told the truth, he might well be looking for another job. All the five men and women are entitled to high security personnel: Cavalcades of cars flashing red and blue lights, screaming sirens to clear the way for them, roadblocks to prevent common citizens straying on to the path of the mighty. I have little doubt that the parking lots in the institute must have been cleared as were the wards through which they passed.

Ask yourself what was the objective of this high-powered exercise? It could not have been the concern for the health of a man they did not know. All they wanted was to show to the people that they were deeply concerned. Not to be left out of the picture, Opposition leaders also turned up at various hospitals to go through the same ritual. If heads of hospitals and clinics want to avoid this VIP nuisance, they have to impose a single regulation: 'No press photographers or TV cameramen are allowed inside the premises.' Once convinced that their visits will get no publicity, the VIPs will automatically stop visiting hospitals and shedding crocodile tears. It is as simple as that.

It would be interesting to know whether any of these VIPs bothered to call on S.S. Sidhu who lost seven members of his family in the Uphaar tragedy. I think not. Sidhu was so crazed with grief that he flailed press photographers and reporters and told them to get out—fast.

28 June 1997

On losing a friend

For many years we were the closest of friends. Our jobs took us to distant cities. Nevertheless, we remained in constant touch. The closeness lasted for over thirty years. Then he turned indifferent and I felt hurt. He was one of the people I wrote about in my *Women and Men in My Life*. He was hurt by what I had to say about him. That had not been my intention. Nevertheless, when I heard of his death on the morning of Sunday, July 6, I was overcome with remorse and sorrow. Our past association haunted me for several days and nights.

Our friendship began in 1932 when we found ourselves in the same class in Government College, Lahore, studying the same subjects and living in the same hostel. Chetan was a very pretty boy: fair, with curly hair and dreamy eyes.

He started seeking my company more to protect himself, not so much because he shared common interests with me. We ate our breakfasts together, attended classes together, played tennis in the afternoons and at least twice a week, went to the movies. During vacations

he went home to Gurdaspur. We wrote to each
other. He was into writing poetry a la Gurudev
Tagore. He sent his compositions to me. It was
soppy stuff, but I was flattered.

Chetan had to count his rupees. One
year he put himself up for election for the
secretaryship of the Hindu-Sikh dining room,
and, as was the custom those days, had cards
printed soliciting votes. I could not understand
why anyone would want to oversee cooking
and feeding arrangements in a college hostel
mess. I discovered that catering contractors
bestowed extra favours to secretaries by not
charging them for meals. The elections were as
fiercely contested as those of the college union.
Chetan won.

After we passed out of college we found
ourselves together in London. I was studying
law; he came to take a shot at the ICS. We both
took the examination. Neither of us made the
grade. Chetan could not afford to stay on in
England and returned home.

We resumed our friendship when I came
back to Delhi: He and Iqbal Singh were the
only two friends I invited to my wedding in
October 1939. A year later, when I set up

practice in Lahore, Chetan spent many months
of the summer in my flat. Though till then he
had not found a job, he was highly successful
in winning the favours of young ladies. His
technique was simple. On hot June afternoons
he would go in his overcoat carrying a single
rose in his hand. When the recipient of the rose
asked him why he was wearing an overcoat,
he would answer 'because it is the only thing I
possess in the world.'

One who fell heavily for this approach
was the ravishing Uma, daughter of Professor
Chatterjee. We celebrated their engagement in
my apartment. That very evening I caught him
flirting with another girl. He was never a one-
woman man. Uma married him, had two sons
and then left him to become Ebrahim Alkazi's
second wife. Chetan shifted to Bombay to try
his luck in films. There he shacked up with
Priya, a good twenty years younger than him.
He did his best to turn her into a film star. He
did not succeed.

Chetan did not make his mark as a director
or an actor as his obituaries now claim. He
made one good film *Neecha Nagar;* the rest
were second-rate, and earned him neither fame

nor money. He did an excellent job reproducing the light and sound show at the Red Fort in Delhi for which I had written the master script in 1965. He got assignments from the Punjab government which he was unable to fulfil.

It was not his successes or failures in the films that affected my affection for him; it was his indifference towards me when I moved to Bombay to take up the editorship of the *Illustrated Weekly of India* in 1969. I was there for a whole of nine years and expected to see a lot of Chetan. I saw something of my other college friends: Balraj Sahni, B.R. Chopra, Kamini Kaushal and even Chetan's own brother Dev Anand. But Chetan, with whom I looked forward to resuming my close friendship, did not bother to contact me even once. Only a month or so before I left Bombay I ran into him and his lady friend at a party. Very airily he said, '*Oi Sardar! Tu milta hee nahin*—O Sardar! You never meet me.' I exploded with anger, '*Besharam!* You shameless creature! Is this the way you fulfil obligations of a forty-year-old friendship?'

His lady friend tried to protest and invited me to come over. 'I don't want to set foot in

your home or see this fellow's face again,'
I replied and stormed out.

Now I regret what I said as I recall Chetan
with tears in my eyes.

19 July 1997

Talk, talk—do nothing

I.K. Gujral mentioned the problem of increasing
population in his first speech in Parliament as
prime minister. Renuka Chaudhury referred
to it in her first interview after taking over
as minister of health. On July 11, full-page
advertisements appeared in all national
newspapers (the cost must have run into
lakhs, if not crores) warning us to face the
truth that if we keep on adding 45,000 baby
boys and girls (thirty-one every minute) to our
population every day, we will have sixteen
million more to feed, clothe, house, educate
and find employment for, every year. We have
been hearing and reading this sort of thing
year after year. And yet we go on breeding
recklessly like rats and rabbits without concern

for the generations to come and the future of the country.

Isn't it time for the government and the political parties to take practical steps to prevent this suicidal lemming's race to damnation? There is only one answer to our population problem: prescribe limits to reproduction and pass a legislation making it compulsory. There will be nothing dictatorial or undemocratic about it if it is passed by our Parliament. The simple provision would be to require every married couple to undergo sterilization after the birth of their second child voluntarily if possible, forcibly if they are reluctant.

At the same time we should disenfranchise all men and women who hereafter have more than two children, and make them non-eligible for all elective posts—from membership of panchayats, zilla parishads, state legislatures, Parliament, right up to those of the Vice-President and President.

This will be a challenging task. But if our leaders are not up to it, they don't deserve to lead the country. Let Renuka Chaudhury take the lead by introducing legislation to this effect in the next session of Parliament. All enlightened Indians will support her and she will win the gratitude of the nation and have her name put down in our history books.

19 July 1997

Laloo's antics

The day Laloo Prasad Yadav finally agreed to step down from the chief ministership of Bihar, I happened to be in Jaipur. I had gone there to speak on problems facing the country. No one was interested in my analysis of the legacy left behind by Pandit Nehru, Indira Gandhi and the prime ministers who followed them. All they wanted was my reaction to Laloo's antics, how a man like him should have been handled and what should be done to him. About his antics, I echoed Harkishen Singh Surjeet's opinion *'drama khel raha bai'*. How he should have been handled, I have no idea. I marvel at his cockiness and arrogance; he never refers to himself as *mein* (I) but *hum*, the royal plural. The way he struts about gives the impression that he is still the *badshah* of Bihar.

Like everyone else, I took sadistic pleasure in
seeing his pride humbled. It is truly said that
'Pride goeth before a fall.' About his having
nominated his wife Rabri Devi as leader of the
party and chief minister of the state, all I could
say was 'how sweet'!

What should be done to Laloo to meet
the ends of justice? That is not for us but for
the courts to decide. If they find him and his
colleagues guilty of the charges framed against
them, they deserve punishment which will
be a lesson to others who may be tempted to
fiddle with public money. But I think it is only
fair that Laloo should not be singled out for
punishment till others against whom similar
charges are still pending for a much longer
time, are tried, absolved or punished. The
Bofors case is still pending, the Hawala scam,
St. Kitts forgery case, Pathak's allegations
against Chandraswamy and Narasimha Rao
and Sukh Ram's unaccounted crores have yet to
reach their final conclusions. At least nineteen
members of Narasimha Rao's government have
still to clear themselves of criminal charges of
large-scale corruption and forgery. Most of all,
Narasimha Rao himself managed to rule the

country for five years by bribing four members of Parliament to switch over to his side to win the crucial vote of confidence. Cases against them have been pending for a much longer time than the fodder scam against Laloo. Unless they are brought to trial first, the inevitable conclusion most people will draw is that they are picking on Laloo Yadav for reasons other than the desire to stamp out corruption.

2 August 1997

Not so golden a jubilee

How does a fifty-year-old man whose vision is so impaired that he cannot see far beyond his nose, who is so hard of hearing that you have to yell words of advice in his ears, who has lost his teeth and can eat only soggy, mushy food, and whose guts have been eaten up by the cancer of corruption, celebrate his birthday? Does he have a chocolate birthday cake with fifty candles lit up before he cuts it? No, he is too asthmatic to blow out all the candles and is too diabetic to eat chocolate and cream. Do his children and grandchildren gather round and sing 'Happy Birthday Bharat Papa, Happy Birthday to you'? No, they do not. They would rather send him to a hospital to get him cured of his many ailments, or perhaps pray that he departs peacefully and lets them manage affairs of the country as best they can. In short, we may well ask ourselves what do we have to celebrate? Why all this hoo-ha when Bharat Papa (or Bharat Mata) is stricken with paralysis and on the verge of death.

Make a quick balance sheet of our achievements and failures and the items on the debit side will far outnumber those on the credit side. On the credit side will be self-sufficiency in food and clothing, and the fact that we have been able to hold together as one nation. On the debit side, a galloping population rate which swallows up whatever we produce from our land and factories: We have learnt to live with shortages of every kind. Not enough schools, colleges, hospitals. Poverty and ignorance, violence and corruption have reached record heights. We have become a nation of one-eyed people led by the totally blind. Let us be more realistic. Instead of crowing over our non-achievements, let us take a hard look at where we went wrong. And instead of talking about it, do something about it.

9 August 1997

Banning and burning books

When books are banned or burnt in public, one or the other of the following excuses are given for doing so: they are politically unacceptable to the government, they offend the religious sentiments of some community, or, they are pornographic. I oppose the proscription or destruction of books on any grounds whatsoever and regard these practices as medieval barbarism unworthy of any society which calls itself civilized. The only proviso I admit is that the State or one's parents have the right to prevent boys and girls below a certain age from being exposed to explicit portrayal of sex in writing or illustrations.

In the middle ages, the Roman Catholic Church not only banned books which went against its cherished beliefs (even though they were irrational), it also burnt them along with their authors. In more recent times, Nazi Germany banned books critical of fascist ideology and forced many authors to flee the country. In present day Communist China, books disapproving of the regime are destroyed and their authors put behind bars. Somewhat worse is the fate of authors living in countries where religious fanatics hold sway as they do in many Islamic nations like Iran, Saudi Arabia, Sudan, Afghanistan, Pakistan and Bangladesh. Not only do they ban books but issue fatwas condemning their authors to death. In India, self-appointed censors of Sikh orthodoxy have not lagged behind; they have summoned scholars, declaring them *tankhaias* to be ostracized from Sikh society, making them recant and undergo punishment.

Books are not banned or burnt in America or Canada, in England or in any European country; they are not banned in Australia or New Zealand. These countries are democracies and they regard the intolerance of views unpalatable to themselves as being undemocratic. So did leaders of our freedom movement, notably Bapu Gandhi and Pandit Nehru. By banning or burning books we do grave disservice to their memory and to the country. If members of our Parliament who indulged in this form of vandalism when they burnt Arun Shourie's book on Ambedkar had thought of the harm they were doing to the country's image, I am sure they would have desisted from doing so. Unfortunately, they only thought of pandering to a certain section of the vote bank. One effect of their thoughtless action will inevitably be an increase in the demand for the book. Truly had Emerson spoken when he said, 'Every burnt book enlightens the world.'

When the British ruled the country, they banned books critical of their Raj, mainly those suspected of preaching Marxism. Among those that fell into their foolish net was Gurudev Tagore's *Red Oleanders* simply because of the word 'Red' in the title. After Independence, our governments took to banning books suspected of blasphemy. They include Aghanand Bharati's *The Ochre Robe*, Aubrey Menon's *Rama Retold*, Wolpert's *Nine Hours to Rama* and Salman Rushdie's *The Satanic Verses*. When I was abroad, I read all of them for the simple reason that they were banned in India. Pandit Nehru was right when he wrote, 'Human nature is notoriously perverse. One has to forbid a thing or taboo it to make it attractive.' He was strongly against State censorship. 'It is dangerous power in the hands of a government: the right to determine what shall be read and what shall not.'

My dear countrymen, read books, criticize them as harshly as you like but raise your voices against the burning or banning of books by the government, the law courts, or an intolerant public.

16 August 1997

Crime and punishment

There are almost as many cases of abduction and extortion of ransom in Delhi as there are in the rest of the country put together. The reason is simple: Delhi is an island of prosperity in the middle of a sea of impoverished villages, with a tradition of robbing the rich. Their ancestors robbed Mughal nobility, their descendants rob the nouveau riche found in abundance in the capital. While those who have been rich for some generations learn not to flaunt their wealth, parvenus display their possessions thus exposing their family members to criminal designs. One recent example was the abduction of ten-year-old Tarun Puri of Golf Links, barely a hundred yards away from where I live. It was carried out in the morning with dozens of people watching. Fortunately, the kidnappers were a bunch of idiots and the police were smart enough to nab them. Tarun is back home unharmed.

A more glaring case was the kidnapping of Ninia Singh on July 19 from the entrance gate of her house in Noida. It took place at 5.30 p.m. and was witnessed by many bystanders. Ninia was hit on the head with an iron rod and pushed into a car. She was driven past police chowkies and the car was refuelled. Though dozens of people saw her lying bleeding on the rear seat of the car, no one came to her rescue. The kidnappers took her to their home. Neither neighbours nor relatives took any notice. 'Yeh to inka roz ka dhanda hai (this is their daily business),' remarked one of the women. Extorting huge sums in ransom has become the way of life of many villages *'Jamna paar'*—across the river—in Ghaziabad district adjoining Delhi.

Ninia was allowed to make two telephone calls requesting ransom. One was on a mobile phone (which can be traced). The other was from a public telephone booth. As instructed, she warned the person on the other end that if the money was not sent, she would be killed. Her abductors lost patience and drove her towards a sugarcane field where they meant to finish her off. Then they had a flat tyre. There were some Muslim farmers working in the fields with a lady and her son supervising their work. While the abductors were busy changing the tyre, Ninia ran out of the car screaming for help. 'Save me, I am a Mussalman. They are going to kill me.' The appeal to communal passions helped. The farmers ran to her help and captured one of her kidnappers. The Muslim lady took Ninia home, cleaned her wounds, fed her and informed the police. Ninia is in fact, a Sikh.

The point for serious consideration is what kind of punishment would fit the crime of abduction and extortion. The immediate response is 'Hang them in public. Jail is not good enough for them.' That, obviously, is not worthy of consideration. Where common people accept a heinous crime as a *dhanda,* and regard abductors as bread-winners (and perhaps heroes), the punishment should be exemplary and designed to disgrace them in the public eye. I am sure if the law is amended and public flogging added to the term in jail, it would have a salutary effect on the crime graph. Parade these gangsters through the lanes of their villages, tie them to trees under which elders of the village meet to gossip and smoke their *hookahs,* pull their pants or dhotis down to their ankles and lash them on their bare buttocks. That will knock out all their bravado and make them objects of ridicule in the society in which they live.

23 August 1997

Blood on their lenses

Though full details of the accident in which Princess Diana, her Egyptian lover and the chauffeur met their deaths in a tunnel are still to be revealed, the Paris police have detained seven press photographers who were chasing her car, and may slap charges of manslaughter on them. However, one thing is quite clear—they had been hounding her ever since her marriage to Prince Charles began to break up. The more she made news because of her love affairs, the hotter became their pursuit. They prowled round her hotel, hired boats to get close to her yacht and followed her car wherever it went. She could not elude them. She was sick and tired of them, and would have wished them dead. The irony of the tragedy is that it was not she who killed them, but they who killed her.

Many celebrities, past and present, have been similarly hounded by press photographers, but none with such savage determination as Princess Diana. Many things contributed to making her the prime target of public voyeurism. She was beautiful, she was a blue-blooded royal, she was utterly candid and kept no secrets. It proved to be a lethal combination of virtues. I do not think there will be another case of homicide by over-exposure for quite some time to come.

Are we in India, in danger of similar kinds of intrusions into the private lives of celebrities? Our film stars are already exposed to this hazard. When they start their careers, they invite publicity. Actresses on the make display their physical assets and enjoy their names being linked with male stars. After they succeed in making the grade, they become very coy. They have no right to complain against press photographers. It is different for politicians and social workers who are in the public eye. Their public life is public property and open to scrutiny of media persons including photographers. Their private lives are not. Though we know many have lady friends and mistresses, as long as it is not reflected in their public conduct in the way of extending patronage to them at public expense, it is strictly their own business. Leave that part of their lives alone.

Book buying

Over a lifetime of buying books in different cities, I have come to the conclusion that it is not the number of books, the air-conditioning or piped music that draws customers towards one bookstore in preference to another, but the personality of the proprietor or the one who attends to customers. Since clients ask for guidance in selecting the best book available on a particular subject, there has to be someone on the staff to help them. But most like to be left alone to browse around and pick up what they want. The proprietor can safely assume that browsers know more about books than him and seek their advice about what he should order from publishers.

In Lahore I used to visit Rama Krishna regularly. Though the proprietor was ill-tempered and quarrelsome, I had no choice as it was the only bookstore in the city. In Chennai, Higginbothams is the largest bookstore. For the years that Prema Subramaniam worked as sales assistant, book buyers flocked to the store because of her. She was well-read and ever-smiling. Today, she continues to smile and sell books for Barnes & Noble in New York. In Pune it was Manneys. In Bombay it was The Strand—small, congested and uncomfortable, but the top favourite of book buyers because the proprietor was knowledgeable and courteous. In Ludhiana it is Lyall, owned by Sunder Dass.

In Delhi I used to visit many bookstores. But with age I have slowed down and end up in Khan Market which is a few steps away from my home. This small market has six bookstores of which the largest and centrally located, is Bahri & Sons. It has more display windows and books that are not available in other shops. But most of all, it is the owner, Balraj Bahri, who has made it a successful venture. Bahri came from Malakwal (Pakistan) as a refugee. He was a man of modest means and education. He did not have the foggiest notion of book buying or selling. He learnt by trial and error. And by a close rapport with his clientele. This year, the Federation of Indian Publishers conferred on him the Distinguished Bookseller Award. It is well deserved.

13 September 1997

The demolished masjid—and after

There is no question that a crime as heinous as the wanton destruction of a place of worship

should be punished. It is an act of villainy and
those who perpetrate it should be treated as
villains. However, I fear very much that the
men and women charged with the demolition
of the Babri Masjid will exploit the trial to
their advantage and portray themselves as
heroes and protectors of the Hindu dharma.
My own gut feeling is that they will succeed in
doing so, and the whole purpose of bringing
them to book will be defeated. Most of those
charged made no secret of their involvement in
the dastardly deed; many of them have gone on
record gloating over what their goondas had
done in Ayodhya. There is serious danger of
miscarriage of justice because of the inordinate
delay in framing charges. We know that in our
country the police and the judiciary move at
snail's pace and trials for murders may take as
long as ten years or more. But more alacrity
could and should have been shown in handling
the Babri Masjid affair. As a matter of fact,
there was no reason why all those who had
instigated the destruction of the mosque were
not apprehended immediately and brought to
trial. They had made many speeches preaching
hatred between the two communities: no more
evidence was needed to ensure their conviction.

Now as things go in our country, a trial against forty-nine accused can be prolonged by months and years. By the time appeals to High Courts and the Supreme Court are concluded, some of the accused may be dead.

Meanwhile, the accused are bound to go round the country extolling their deeds and to get political mileage. It is incumbent on the media and our countrymen to strongly countenance such propaganda. By breaking that one derelict mosque, they have disgraced the fair name of Hinduism so rightly proud of its tradition of tolerance. They must not be allowed to get away with this kind of vandalism.

27 September 1997

Morning blues

There was a time when I rose very early at the ambrosial hour *(amritvela)* to start the day with prayer. That was over half a century ago. Then I came to the conclusion that prayer did no one any good (even goondas and politicians pray for success) and I could use the same time more fruitfully than waste it mumbling hymns in praise of the Almighty. So, though I continue to rise very early, I begin my day reading the morning paper which is delivered to me at 4.30 a.m. Then I watch news on TV. There are quite a few channels to choose from: Zee, BBC, CNN, Doordarshan and Star. With dawn and the cawing of crows, I am saturated with knowledge of what is going on in my country and the world. Last few mornings I have also been watching interviews with party leaders and proceedings at the two houses of Parliament.

Now I conclude that even if prayer does not do much good to anyone, at least it is not depressing. Reading newspapers and watching TV leaves me in a black mood for the rest of the day. Watching the pandemonium created by MPs in the Rajya Sabha when Prime Minister I.K. Gujral presented the Jain Commission report, I concluded that we were not fit for the Western kind of democracy. And hearing Sitaram Kesri's impassioned plea to Sonia Gandhi to take over the reins of the Congress party ('She and only she can save the party,' he said, thumping the rostrum to loud applause from his partymen), I felt perhaps some form of monarchy would suit us better.

'Kesriji,' I said to myself, 'if you are pinning your hopes on reviving the Nehru-Gandhi dynasty through an Italian-domiciled Indian lady who always had great disdain for politics and threatened to divorce her pilot husband when he reluctantly entered it, you might well have contemplated asking Queen Elizabeth when she visited India, to stay on and give us the kind of government her ancestors had imposed on us.' If it can be the Turin-born Sonia, why not a blue-blooded Brit named Elizabeth born in London? It is truly pathetic.

I am seriously considering giving up reading newspapers and watching TV altogether and resuming prayer; this time not for myself but for my country.

29 November 1997

•

The poor have more fun

Shashi Tharoor, author of *The Great Indian Novel* (a parody inspired by the *Mahabharat*) and *India: From Midnight to the Millennium*, works with the UN in New York. He is of the opinion that poorer the nation, the more holidays it has. According to Tharoor's 'Holiday Index', although India is not yet the poorest in the world, it is certainly on top of the list of holiday makers. Our next-door neighbours, Pakistan, China, Burma and Sri Lanka, though marginally better off than us, do not have as many *chhuttees* as we; nor do Bhutan or Bangladesh which are poorer than us. I think the main reason for their having fewer holidays is that all of them are single-religion states—Islamic, Hindu or Buddhist. Ours is a multi-religious society in which each religious group clamours for national holidays on their festivals. So our supine governments have declared forty-four official holidays, ranging from the secular (like Independence and Republic days) to birthdays of founders of religions, sects and sub-sects. Birthdays of Jain Mahavir, the Buddha, Christ, Prophet Mohammed, Guru Nanak, Guru Gobind Singh, Guru Ravidas and Valmiki are national holidays. We have added Mahatma Gandhi's birthday to the list.

Being a predominantly Hindu country, Hindu holidays predominate. They include Diwali, Holi, Mahashivratri and Ganesh Chaturthi. Muslims have their three Eids: Eid-e-Milad-un-Nabi (the Prophet's birthday), Eid-ul-Fitr (the *badee* Eid following Ramadan) and Eid-ul-Zoha or Bakri Eid. They also have Muharram—a largely Shia festival. Christians have, besides Christmas, Easter and Good Friday. Sikhs, in addition to the two Gurus' birthdays, have martyrdom anniversaries of their fifth and ninth Gurus as well as Baisakhi. Parsis have their New Year's Day (Navroz). The list is almost as long as the days in the year.

To start with, we have 104 weekends. Government servants are entitled to annual leave, casual leave, compassionate leave and sick leave (a fake certificate from an amenable medico will do). Then we shut the offices if the boss kicks the bucket. One can always rely on *bandhs*, strikes and lockouts to add a few more days of no-work. As it is, we have a large population who avoid work altogether—such are our sadhus, godmen and godwomen. Also, men and women who believe that the purpose of life is to achieve peace of mind through prayer or meditation. In fact, we are a bone-lazy nation: religion provides us plenty of excuses to evade work and wallow in idleness. With this attitude towards life, we are never likely to catch up with the advanced nations of the world nor become prosperous. We will remain the authors of our poverty.

20 December 1997

India's Man of Destiny

There is a general consensus that the man most suited to be the next prime minister of India is Atal Behari Vajpayee. He has been prime minister once but was not given enough time to prove his mettle. The post may still elude him, but most people among whom I count myself, are in agreement that he, more than any other leader deserves to be put back in the saddle. He is clean: no breath of scandal is attached to his name. Being a bachelor, he is not likely to indulge in nepotism nor let his relatives take advantage of his position. If he has any cronies, I have not heard of them. Personally, he is above communal prejudices and has never been known to make statements that may hurt the religious feelings of any community.

He is an able man; a man of letters, a poet and an aesthete well above most of our rabble-rousing politicians of today. He has several collections of poems to his credit—some of them have been set to music. No other prime minister since Nehru (who only wrote in English) can lay claim to a place in Indian literature as can Vajpayee.

Vajpayee is a farsighted statesman and is not known to compromise his principles for immediate gains. He proved his ability as foreign minister and as member of the Indian delegation to numerous international conferences. And he is the very best orator of Hindi we have heard since Independence. It is a treat to hear him speak: no mob oratory, no rhetoric, only well-reasoned arguments couched in the most elegant prose, pauses at the right places, ending in never-to-be-forgotten punchlines.

Vajpayee is a courteous, polished gentleman who keeps his cool at all times, and is never known to be rude to anyone. In short, he is a most likeable, loveable character.

There is only one minus point in Vajpayee's curriculum vitae—the political party over which he presides. It is tarnished with anti-Muslim and anti-Christian prejudices. I know for certain that he does not share these prejudices. Soon after the destruction of the Babri Masjid, at a small private gathering, he read out a poem he had composed on his birthday, 25th December. In no uncertain terms it expressed deep anguish over what had happened at Ayodhya and explained his silence through a refrain 'Have I really become old?' I could understand the constraints that compelled him to keep his thoughts to himself. But it was evident that he realized that although India is a predominantly Hindu state, it is not a Hindu but a secular state in which religious minorities expect equal treatment. I hope and pray that if and when he does become prime minister of the country—as I expect and pray he will—he will distance himself from men and women who have given Hindutva an ugly image.

27 December 1997

Looking forward to 1998

The past year, our cup of misery was filled to the brim. A lot of good people died and a lot of rotters came out of the cold to grab centre stage. The most depressing event of last year was the Congress party ditching the Government on a flimsy excuse, thereby forcing mid-term elections. Its unprincipled action calculated solely by Sitaram Kesri to make a bid for prime ministership encouraged sundry politicians to ditch parties in which they felt they had no future, to look for greener pastures elsewhere. In every case it was gross opportunism. We saw it in Uttar Pradesh, where a group of MLAs of different parties were made ministers of a BJP government en bloc. We lost the little respect we had for these legislators and were disenchanted with the BJP's assumptions of political morality: when it comes to principles, it is no better than the others.

Then followed a spate of desertions from the Congress, by politicians who sensed that their chances of being re-elected to Parliament were bleak. So they had many nasty things to say about Kesri and much praise for their new-found leaders. To describe them as rats deserting a sinking ship would be grossly defamatory to the rodents. No doubt we will see a lot more of this sort of thing in the next month or two, till the elections are over. There is a good chance of it continuing even afterwards if the electorate does not give a clear verdict in favour of one party. At the moment, this seems unlikely.

However, one has to admit that the only ones who have not sullied their reputation by compromising with their Marxist principles are the Communists. Unfortunately, their presence is limited to just three states—West Bengal, Tripura and Kerala. The prospects of their extending their influence are not very bright.

Will Sonia Gandhi's entering the political arena make much difference? It would be foolish to hazard a guess because so far she has remained behind the screen as an enigmatic figure. In her favour are her youth, good looks and family charisma. Against her are her foreign origin and her aversion to, and lack of experience in politics. Hanging above her like the sword of Damocles is the Bofors deal in which her late husband's name is implicated. The BJP spokeswoman has openly proclaimed that these negative points will be highlighted during their election campaign. Sonia will have her first taste of the nastiness of (Indian) politics. I do not think she will be able to stand up to it for too long.

We do not have very much to look forward to this year: a change of government, of course; perforce, a change in the dramatis personae. Change in the character of our leaders? Not likely. All said and done, they are drawn from our midst. And we have become a second-rate people.

Not wanted anywhere

The population of people forced to leave their homes in fear of losing their lives has reached the highest figure recorded in history. The UN Office of the High Commissioner for Refugees in Delhi estimates that it is looking after over twenty-six million men, women and children in 123 countries. I am pretty certain that the total number of refugees is even higher. Take the case of India. We have a long history of people from foreign lands coming to seek asylum and being accommodated. We had Jews who settled largely in Maharashtra, Kerala and in big cities like Calcutta. We had Parsis fleeing Muslim persecution in Iran. They were welcomed by the rulers of Gujarat and are now settled largely in Mumbai. We had mass migrations of non-Muslims from West and East Pakistan, estimated at over ten million in 1947.

In the 1960s we had over 100,000 Tibetans including the Dalai Lama fleeing Chinese persecution and seeking sanctuary in India. They are still with us. We had more than ten million Hindus fleeing East Pakistan between 1969 and 1970; not all of them returned to Bangladesh. The same happened to the 200,000 Tamils who fled Sri Lanka—100,000 remain in Tamil Nadu. Recently we had 56,000 Chakma tribals migrating from Bangladesh to Tripura—they have been persuaded to return to their homes. We also had Afghans (over 50,000) and similar numbers from Iran, Sudan and Somalia. The UNHCR estimate of foreign refugees living in India today is around 2,75,000.

In addition to all this, we have Indians displaced from one region moving to another.

During Bhindranwale's time and Khalistani terrorism, many Hindus moved their families from the Punjab to Haryana or Delhi. After the anti-Sikh violence following Indira Gandhi's assassination, several Sikh families settled in other parts of India returned to Punjab. And most recently, thousands of Kashmiri Pandits fled the Valley of Jhelum and migrated to Jammu and other cities in India.

One significant difference between refugees who came to India and refugees in neighbouring countries is that while we were able to rehabilitate and reintegrate them, our neighbours are still having problems in doing so. No one in India uses the word 'refugee' for people who are in fact refugees; in Pakistan, Indian Muslims who migrated there fifty years ago are still known as *mohajareens,* and local Muslims don't encourage intermarriage with them. Perhaps this is due to our age-old tradition of welcoming people no longer welcome in their own countries. Pakistanis and Bangladeshis have still to open their hearts to people who seek refuge with them.

10 January 1998

Why Indian Muslims don't count

Despite India having the second largest population of Muslims in the world—larger than in Pakistan or all the Arab countries put together—Pakistan has successfully kept Indian Muslims out of international Muslim organizations. And despite India's active support to the Palestinian cause against Israel, whenever the Kashmir issue comes up in international fora, Muslim countries follow the dictates of Pakistan and vote against India. It is a sad commentary on our foreign policy. Or is it that though Muslim countries are often at loggerheads with each other, whenever one is confronted with a non-Muslim country like India, Israel or Greece, they close ranks and, regardless of the merits of the dispute, act in unison against them?

It can be statistically established that Muslims have shed more Muslim blood fighting each other than non-Muslims have in their wars against Muslim countries. In recent times, Iraq waged an eight-year war against Iran and annexed Kuwait for a short time. It could be established that Saddam Hussein of

Iraq has killed more Muslims than anyone in the history of the world. Nevertheless, he remains 'hero number one' of the Muslim world. In Afghanistan, a seemingly endless civil war has been raging for ten years. The Taliban who claim to represent true Islamic values are backward-looking bigots and have brought disgrace to the fair name of Islam. The only country openly supporting them is Pakistan.

We have to understand the dilemmas and contradictions of the Islamic world before secular India and her Muslims can decide how to cope with their predicament.

17 January 1998

Gandhi vs Godse

In a few days it will be the fiftieth anniversary of Bapu Gandhi's assassination. Three bullets fired by Nathuram Godse on January 30, 1948 ended his life. It should be borne in mind that before opening fire, Godse touched Bapu's feet to ask for his forgiveness for what he was about to do—even *he* recognized the fact that his victim was no ordinary mortal but a Mahatma: a great soul venerated throughout the world. Godse had no personal grievance against him but felt that what the Mahatma stood for had done harm to the country and he should therefore be eliminated. He had no fear that he would have to pay the price for his deed with his own life (which he did when he was hanged to death).

On January 30, we will hear a lot of platitudes about the relevance of Mahatma Gandhi's teachings. A lot of lip-worship will be paid to him and flowers will be strewn on his *samadhi* to the chanting of his favourite hymns *'Vaishnav jan to tainey kahiye'* and *'Raghupati Raaghav Raja Ram'*. But when we search our souls, we will be forced to admit that little or nothing of the Gandhi legacy remains with us. We started frittering it away the day after he was killed, and have continued to do so ever since. When we allowed the Babri Masjid in Ayodhya to be reduced to rubble, we finally buried Gandhi's ashes as well. As Gandhi's star dipped into the Indian Ocean, Godse's star rose in the Indian skies.

Is there any hope of resurrecting Gandhi's legacy? I have been pondering over this question for many days, because despite being an iconoclast, an agnostic and a drinking man who rejects a lot of Bapu's ideas on religion, prohibition, celibacy and nature cure, I call myself a Gandhian. I have come to the conclusion that another Kurukshetra will be fought in the general elections due in another few weeks, between the remnants of Gandhism on the one side ranged against Godseism on the other. At first sight, my analysis of the issues involved at the elections may appear naive and simplistic to you, but ponder over it and you may come round to my point of view.

Do not go by what leaders of different political parties say. When it comes to Gandhism versus Godseism, all of them will profess to be on the side of Gandhism (I exclude the Communists from this dispute because they have always kept aloof from this particular issue). As I see it, the Sangh Parivar are upholders of Godseism; those ranged against it, however poor their track record in this context, are for Gandhism. If the Sangh Parivar prevail, we may as well forget that we

ever had a Gandhi in our midst. If the parties
aligned against the Parivar carry the polls,
we may still be able to revive the Gandhi we
murdered fifty years ago.

24 January 1998

A forgetful nation

'There were no villages in pre-Partition India
where Muslims and Sikhs lived like brothers.
Did you ever see one or did you make one up
to fit into the theme of your story?'

This was the first question shot at me. The
second was, 'Is it true that during the partition
killings of the summer of 1947, trainloads of
corpses were sent across the Indo-Pakistan
border? Or is it a figment of your imagination
which you used to fit into the theme of your
story?'

For good measure, a third man described
my novel *Train to Pakistan* as 'no more than a
political thriller'.

The question-and-answer session took
place at a press conference the day following

the screening of the film adaptation of *Train
to Pakistan* (directed by Pamela Rooks) at the
International Film Festival at Siri Fort. The
auditorium was packed to overflowing. Many
in the audience who had lived through the
partition were in tears. Those who had only
heard about the horrors from their parents
seemed unconvinced that such things could
indeed have taken place.

I found the reaction of the audience
heart-warming. What depressed me were
the questions put to me by journalists whom
I expected to be better informed. Have we
already forgotten the price that both India and
Pakistan had to pay for our Independence, in
loss of lives and suffering?

The Jews the world over have never let
anyone forget what Adolf Hitler and his Nazis
did to them during World War II. Hundreds
of books have been written on the subject;
dozens of films have been made depicting
the Holocaust. Prison camps where Jews
were shot or gassed to death have become
places of pilgrimage. There are museums in
Germany and Israel that display relics of Nazi
brutalities against Jews. But we Indians and

Pakistanis have chosen to forget what we did to each other to gain our freedom. We have no museums, no memorials to commemorate what was undoubtedly one of the greatest tragedies in recorded history. The uprooting of ten million people from their homes, the loss of one million lives, rape and abduction of thousands of women have all been swept under the carpet of oblivion. In sheer magnitude what Chenghis Khan, Ghazni, Nadir Shah and Abdali put together did not do, we did within a period of three months.

Should the partition be remembered? Has it any relevance to us today? My answer to both questions is an emphatic 'yes'. We must not forget that the partition did in fact happen and can happen again. That is why I keep reminding people who clamour for an independent Kashmir, Khalistan or Nagaland to remember what happened to Muslims when some of them asked for a separate Muslim state. I keep telling my fellow Sikhs that the worst enemies of the Khalsa Panth are Khalistanis, and of the Nagas, those who ask for an independent Nagaland. Reminding ourselves of what happened in 1947 and realizing the possibilities of the events recurring, we should resolve that we will never let history repeat itself.

31 January 1998

Fingers on the pulse

Delhi once had a *nabeena* (blind) hakeem sahib who diagnosed his patients' ailments by simply feeling their pulses. It is assumed that we journalists also have our fingers on the pulse of the nation and decipher which way and in what strength its blood is flowing. Evidently we do not have the skills of the blind healer of Delhi, as we seem to have gone grievously wrong in our assessment of Sonia Gandhi. Her entry into active politics took all of us by surprise. We then proceeded to underrate her impact on the people. She is evidently drawing larger crowds than any other political leader. We still hold that people who throng to her meetings come out of sheer curiosity, they are *tamashaees,* idle spectators; and they should not be counted as voters for the Congress party. We may again be proved wrong.

What we of the Indian media failed to take into account is the innate respect the masses have for ruling families. Starting with Kashmir, we have the Abdullahs—Sheikh Sahib, Farooq and now his son. Himachal Pradesh: Virbhadra Singh, a princeling and his Rani Sahiba. Punjab: Parkash Singh Badal, a rich zamindar and his extended clan of land-owning Jats. Haryana: Devi Lal, Bansi Lal and Bhajan Lal, their sons, nephews and grandsons. Uttar Pradesh: Kumaon Brahmins—Pandes, Pants and Joshis, Sanjay Singh of Amethi, Dinesh Singh's wife and relations. Bihar: the upstart leader Laloo, his wife Rabri Devi and her brothers. Orissa: the Patnaiks. Madhya Pradesh: Digvijay Singh (big zamindar), Madhavrao Scindia of Gwalior and the Shukla brothers. Maharashtra: Bal Thackeray, his son and nephew.

The southern states have spawned a new breed of leaders who have graduated from film studios to Vidhan Sabhas and Parliament. In Tamil Nadu we had M.G. Ramachandran and now his protégé Jayalalitha. In Andhra Pradesh: N.T. Rama Rao, his widow and his son-in-law Chandrababu Naidu. The pattern is roughly the same: one man makes a power base and rises to leadership; his kith and kin ride piggyback on him to ascend the political ladder. What is more incredible is that the common Indian thinks that this is as it ought to be. So one should not be surprised with the impact Sonia Gandhi has made since she discarded the veil. The boat of the Sangh Parivar riding high on the crest of the wave of popularity may very well flounder on the rock of the Nehru-Gandhi dynasty.

14 February 1998

Politics divorced from morality

Politics and morality do not go together. This is the first lesson that our recent elections have once again made abundantly clear. Every single person known to me who was in the fray told me the same things: those who lost said they had been betrayed by their partymen and were beaten not by their opponents but by people who swore to help them. If this is true, as it seems to be, we cannot help but come to the conclusion that we have become a nation of face-flatterers and back-stabbers.

Another equally distressing conclusion is that we no longer look upon corruption as grounds for disqualification when it comes to holding political posts. Or perhaps we no longer believe that a person charged with corruption is in fact guilty—unless he is convicted by a court of law. And since our courts of law are never in a hurry to pronounce judgements, those charged with crimes enter electoral frays, as if they had done nothing wrong. And more often than not, they win. So we have Jayalalitha staging a spectacular comeback, Sukh Ram demolishing the Congress party in Himachal Pradesh, Laloo Prasad Yadav cocking a snook at his denigrators, and Balram Jakhar, Buta Singh and Sanjay Singh returning to the Lok Sabha.

Party-hopping is no longer regarded as an act leading to expulsion; it is no longer even frowned upon. Uttar Pradesh MLAs set the example with a sizeable chunk of Mayawati's supporters going over en bloc to Kalyan Singh. Of them, the most distinguished party-hopper, Naresh Aggarwal, made three hops in one week. Dr Subramaniam Swamy's switching over from being the prime accuser and

persecutor of Jayalalitha, to swearing fealty
to her and becoming her candidate as finance
minister left me breathless with surprise. As did
Kumaramangalam junior who, like his father,
was an ardent socialist a few years ago, and is
today an equally ardent Bhajpaite.

Less fortunate was a very young friend,
Mani Shankar Aiyar. He built his political
career riding on the shoulders of Rajiv Gandhi.
He continued his close association with the
erstwhile first family headed by Sonia Gandhi
and the Congress. When he saw the Congress
ship skippered by Sitaram Kesri going down,
he quit the Congress and sought the patronage
of Jayalalitha. When that failed, he tried
Mamata Banerjee and Subhas Ghising. When
he found no takers, he fought the elections as
an independent candidate and lost. He is now
back with the Congress.

The same fate befell Suresh Kalmadi. From
a passionate critic of the Congress, he turned
into a Congress supporter, becoming a protégé
of Sharad Pawar who always stayed with
Kalmadi when he was in Delhi. Kalmadi ditched
his mentor, fought the elections independently
against the Congress and was humbled.

To me, the most distressing feature of the recent elections was the resurgence in belief in astrology, horoscopes and other unscientific methods of forecasting the future. I cannot understand how otherwise highly intelligent people can subscribe to this kind of hocus-pocus which has time and again proved to be just that. The list of eminent Indians who swear by the configuration of planets makes impressive reading.

There is Narasimha Rao who consults his *jyotishi* to fix even the time and date for the release of his book. Jayalalitha, Subramaniam Swamy and Dr Karan Singh have the assurances of their horoscopes that they will become prime ministers of India. Jakhar and Buta Singh also believe in the occult. The latest is BJP leaders succumbing to the prediction that ill-luck has dogged them because, according to *vaastu shastra*, the entrance gate of their office faces the wrong direction. So Murli Manohar Joshi and K.B. Malkani had it shut and another one opened on the side.

Thus, the recent elections have proved that we have not only expunged morality from our politics, we are also declining into mental sickness. We are getting onto the back of the donkey of irrational superstition hoping to ride into the twenty-first century.

I am reminded of a *shloka* in the *Atharva Veda:*

Triya Charitram
Manushya Bhagyam
Devo na Jaanati

(Of the character of a woman
And the fate of a man
Even the gods are ignorant.)

28 March 1998

The inimitable R.K. Laxman

Long before I got to know him, I had sensed that Laxman had a touch of the genius. I had sent a story, 'Man, How does the Government of India Run?' to the then editor of the *Illustrated Weekly of India,* C.R. Mandy. He sent the story to Laxman for a suitable illustration. Without ever having seen me or my photograph, Laxman drew a caricature of a Sikh clerk (who was the main character of my story) and it bore a startling resemblance to me.

By then he had established the reputation of being India's best cartoonist and most people took the *Times of India* because of his front-page cartoons and its last-page crossword puzzle. The rest of the paper was like any other national daily. And however distinguished its editors, few people bothered with the contents of its edit page.

I knew Laxman was the youngest of R.K. Narayan's six brothers. His illustrations of his brother's short stories put life into the narrative and highlighted the fact that they were Tamil Brahmins settled in Mysore. We struck up a close friendship almost from the first day I took up the editorship of the *Illustrated Weekly of India*. I told him that in my opinion he was the world's greatest cartoonist. I meant it because I had lived in England, the USA and France for many years and seen the works of cartoonists there. Laxman did not protest: he evidently agreed with my assessment of his worth. Almost every other morning he came to my room and asked me to order coffee for him. He never bothered to ask me if I was busy. Far from resenting his dropping in unannounced, I looked forward to the gossip sessions. However, while he thought nothing of wasting my time every other morning, he never allowed anyone to enter his cabin while he was at work.

Laxman was as witty a raconteur of people's foibles as he was adept in sketching them on paper. I discovered that he was a bit of a snob and did not deign to talk to the junior staff. My son Rahul once told me that he had run into Laxman at a cinema. When Laxman discovered that Rahul was not in the most expensive seats, he ticked him off.

He was a great socialiser and could be seen at cocktail parties of consulates, the rich and the famous. He loved driving through congested streets and gladly accepted my invitations for drinks, driving all the way from Malabar Hills where he lived, to Colaba, five miles away from my flat. Unlike his brother who was abstemious, Laxman loved his Scotch. It had to be of premium quality. However, he never returned the hospitality. Other characteristics

I noticed about him which he shared with his brother was an exaggerated respect for money. R.K. Narayan was the doyen of Indian authors. He drove a hard bargain.

Once when AIR invited ten of India's top authors to talk about their work and offered what seemed to be more than adequate fees, Narayan accepted only on the condition that he be given at least one rupee more than the others. Likewise, Laxman and I were asked by Manjushri Khaitan of the B.K. Birla family to produce commemoration volumes on Calcutta's 300th anniversary. We were given five-star accommodation. I accepted whatever Manjushri offered me for writing the text. Laxman demanded and got, twice as much. His cartoons sold many more copies than my book did.

Underneath the façade of modesty, both Narayan and Laxman conceal enormous amounts of self-esteem and inflated egos. Once again I have to concede that neither has anything to be modest about. They are at the top in their respective fields.

5 September 1998

Kakar's *Ascetic of Desire*

The silliest and most unscientific book on sex that I have ever read is Vatsayana's *Kamasutra*. There is no basis whatsoever for his having divided men and women into categories according to the size of their genitals. Vatsayana's categorization of males into hares, horses and bulls, and women into gazelles, mares and elephants which was basic to his analysis of the man-woman physical relationship, is entirely arbitrary. So is his penchant for enumerating just about every action that brought men and women closer to each other. For him, the number 64 has some kind of mystical significance. Following Manu, he listed transgressions of the caste code by the four *varnas* to a total of sixty-four. How seriously can anyone accept this kind of treatise today? The *Kamasutra* is not even good pornography; it is downright silly and often hilarious. The one thing that can be said in its favour is that it was compiled sometime around the fourth century AD during the so-called Golden Age of the Gupta Empire, and gives the reader some idea of the free and open society of those times. It was also the time when erotic sculpture and painting flourished in different parts of the country.

Not much is known about the author of the *Kamasutra* besides his name and that he lived in Kausambi and Varanasi and had access to the court of the ruling prince. Using extracts from his treatise, Sudhir Kakar, India's leading psychoanalyst, has reconstructed his life and times. He has done so with the consummate skill of a master craftsman using psycho-analytic techniques, imagination and felicitous prose to bring to life a scholar of ancient erotica who died over 1500 years ago. He uses an ingenious device of getting a young neophyte (obviously himself) who spends many days over many years in Vatsayana's hermitage on the pretext of writing a commentary on the *Kamasutra*. He questions Vatsayana on contentious points like the art of seduction, foreplay etc.

If Kakar is right, Vatsayana was an illegitimate child of a wealthy tradesman and brought up in an establishment of courtesans run by two sisters, one of whom was his father's mistress. Young Vatsayana became a favourite of his *mausi* (aunt). He saw the comings and goings of rich patrons who came to see the girls sing and dance. After a *gurukul* schooling, he gained access to the ruler's court and was granted a stipend to compile a definitive work on erotic arts. He was married off to the ruler's beautiful but wayward sister-in-law many years younger than him. They retired to a hermitage at the fringe of a forest. While the Acharya was busy writing or meditating, his wife loitered around in the jungle watching birds and beasts and contemplated on life by a lily pond. On this sylvan scene arrived a young man to compile a biography of the Acharya and clarify some points of his magnum opus. After their midday meal, while the Acharya was resting, the young student followed his guru's wife into the forest. They became lovers. One day the Acharya came upon them and caught them. He said nothing but disappeared for ever. The young lovers fled the hermitage and the town because an extramarital relationship between a *shishya* and the guru's wife was regarded the gravest of sins. They had an illegitimate child. In short, the author of the *Kamasutra,* the Hindu classic on sex, was himself, impotent.

31 October 1998

Day of rejoicing

I look forward to Republic Day. So, I expect, does everyone else. Unfortunately for most of us it remains a spectacle performed by others, watched by us. We are not participants but mere spectators. In my younger days I used to watch the march past consisting of bands, tanks, armoured vehicles, missiles, floats, folk dancers, caparisoned elephants, camels and school children. But I haven't watched them now for over twenty years. No one sends me a pass and I don't feel like blowing up Rs 200 to watch something that I can with greater comfort ensconced in my armchair by the fireside, facing my TV set. Much as I enjoy what I see, I remain an outsider. That saddens me, because this is the one day in the year we should be celebrating in our homes and in the homes of our relatives and friends, exchanging gifts and making merry. The Government has hijacked Republic Day and turned it into a purely *sarkari* extravaganza.

Is there another day in the year that we can convert into a day of national rejoicing? One that readily comes to mind is Independence

Day, August 15. Unfortunately, that day has also been appropriated by the Government with the prime minister delivering his speech from the Red Fort and everyone making balance sheets of our achievements and failures. In any case, it is not the best time of the year for any kind of festivity.

After eliminating religious festivals for obvious reasons, the most suitable day I can think of is Gandhi's birthday, October 2. The weather is clement, there are no sectarian overtones to the event and all said and done, he was, and is, our Bapu. All we need is to build up a consensus on making it our truly national day of rejoicing.

Fatwa on Rushdie

The lesson to be learnt from Ayatollah Khomeini's fatwa passing the sentence of death on Salman Rushdie for writing *The Satanic Verses* is that nothing boosts sales of a book more as banning it or vilifying its author. Not many people would have read this book but for the worldwide brouhaha

created over it following the ban imposed
by the Indian Government and all Muslim
countries. Attacks on British and American
culture centres, burning copies of the book in
public places, rioting mobs quelled by police
opening fire only added to the book's sales.
The Satanic Verses remained in the top of the
list of bestsellers in English-speaking countries
for many months. Few, very few people were
able to plod through more than fifty pages of
the over-500 paged book, but owning a copy
became a status symbol. If you want to know
more about Salman Rushdie, a summary of
his most controversial novel and the reception
it got, you can do no better than read *The
Rushdie Affair: The Novel, The Ayatollah and
the West* by Daniel Pipes. It is published by Sita
Ram Goel's *Voice of India.*

The author, Daniel Pipes, is a specialist
on the Islamic world with a doctorate from
Harvard University. Besides the reception *The
Satanic Verses* got, Pipes gives us some details
of Rushdie's life. He was born in Bombay in
June 1947, the only son of four children of non-
Kashmiri-speaking Kashmiri parents. They
were evidently prosperous, as after a few years

of Cathedral School in Bombay, he was sent to
Rugby and then to King's College, Cambridge.
He specialized in Islamic history.

On his return home, the family migrated
to Karachi. Salman could not come to terms
with the stifling atmosphere in Pakistan
and decided that if it could not be Bombay,
it would be London. Even in England he
found the discrimination practised by Whites
against Asians and Blacks unacceptable. *The
Satanic Verses* has quite a lot to say about
the vandalism of punks and skinheads against
a Bangladeshi family running a restaurant.
Rushdie took British citizenship, married an
English girl, Clarissa, and has a son (Zafar)
by her. He divorced Clarissa and married an
American novelist, Marianne Wiggins. This
marriage had begun to come apart before the
publication of *The Satanic Verses*. After the
fatwa, Marianne stood by Salman for a month
but could not take the strain of remaining in
hiding with a man who had a huge price on his
head, and divorced him.

Rushdie continues to be hunted by
Muslim fanatics and remains under heavy
security provided by the British Government.

He has become the symbol of defiance against religious bigotry and the right of freedom of expression. The ban on *The Satanic Verses* spawned a lot of wrong notions about its contents in the minds of people who had not read it. Most of them think that the title applies to the entire *Koran*. It does not. It is taken from two very brief lines diluting Islam's total rejection of idolatry. They are said to have been dictated not by Allah but by Satan, and later withdrawn. However, Rushdie *does* question the Muslim belief that the *Koran* was revealed to Prophet Mohammed by Allah. He is also very irreverent in his attitude towards the Prophet and his wives. Rushdie has a penchant for hurting people's deepest sentiments. It is ironic that his name, 'Rushdie' is derived from the Arabic word for 'mature', 'reasonable' and 'proper'. It is not surprising that *The Satanic Verses* has become 'highly valued contraband' in countries that have imposed a ban on it. It has been translated into Arabic and is available in Arab-Muslim countries at a very high price. In Turkey it is available under the counter at $200 (Rs 8500). Such is human nature. As soon as you forbid anything, it becomes all the more desirable.

30 January 1999

Who are you trying to fool?

You can fool some people for some time, but you can't fool all the people all the time. Our present-day rulers think they can. They are in for a very unpleasant surprise: no one believes a word of what they say. Take the latest case of the brutal murders of the Australian missionary working among lepers in Orissa and his two infant sons. The police have identified the leader of the gang that perpetrated the crime as being an active member of the Bajrang Dal. The long, white-bearded Giriraj Kishore had the audacity to proclaim on TV channels that there are no lepers in that area. A few minutes later the same TV channels showed pictures of lepers grieving over the loss of the man who had devoted his entire life looking after them. Who is lying—Giriraj Kishore or the lepers? You decide for yourself.

While the investigating authorities had named the principal killer as a member of the Bajrang Dal, Home Minister L.K. Advani, to whose *parivar* Bajrang Dal belongs, gives the Dal a clean chit. Who knows the facts better, the men on the spot or the home minister in Delhi committed to preserving the image of his *parivar* as one happy family? You decide for yourself.

And finally, the prime minister sends a committee of three cabinet ministers—Murli Manohar Joshi, George Fernandes (the giant killer of yesteryear) and Patnaik—to go to Orissa, investigate and give him a report. They spend about an hour or so 'investigating'. Neither Joshi nor Fernandes can speak Oriya, but along with the effete-looking Patnaik (it is hard to believe he is Biju Patnaik's son), they proclaim that the killers were in no way connected to the *parivar* and it was all a big conspiracy to defame the government. Can you believe a word of what they say?

The trail of falsehood goes back to the victimization of Christian institutions in Gujarat and violence against the nuns in Madhya Pradesh. We are glibly told that Christians have invited trouble on themselves by converting tribals to their faith. Furthermore, they are funded by the substantial donations they receive from abroad. But of course they are; they need modern equipment for the hundreds of hospitals, clinics and leper homes they run. And their schools and colleges, unlike most others, are not money-making shops. They don't buy converts; they don't bully people to convert— only they accept Christianity who feel a sense of gratitude for what Christian institutions have done for them. I am pretty certain that Prime Minister Atal Behari Vajpayee, Madan Lal Khurana and Bansi Lal do not accept the 'official' versions put out periodically; otherwise they would not be fasting at Gandhi's *samadhi* on the anniversary of his martyrdom. Thank God we still have some people with a conscience to lead us.

6 February 1999

Changing times

It's been a hard, long winter—the longest and hardest within living memory. Never before do

I recall Delhi being under a blanket of fog from a week before Christmas right up to the first week of February. Come to think of it, I can't recall a single foggy day till a few years after Independence.

I've known colder days in Delhi but for very short spells—no more than four or five days when the water in the marble fountain in the garden froze to ice. But the days were crisp and clear with blue skies and bright sunshine. Above all, the air was always fresh. The nights were still and silent. We knew the progress of the moon from the crescent to its fullness. On moonless nights, the sky was studded with myriads of stars.

We saw meteors break loose from their moorings and disappear into the unknown. We gazed at the constellations we knew and could guess the time from the position of Great Bear around the Pole Star. The only noises that slightly disturbed our early slumbers were the howling of jackals near garbage dumps and the calls of night watchmen shouting to each other, 'khabardar ho!' There were no policemen on patrol duties. Thefts and robberies were rare occurrences.

All that has changed. No jackals howl, no watchmen call out to each other. Police vans scamper about throughout the night. On an average there are four to five cases of theft, robbery, rape and murder every twenty-four hours. Worst of all is the change in climate. To breathe fresh air, you have to go twenty miles or more beyond the city limits. To see the stars and the moon, you have to go even further because city and village lights have robbed us of nature's gift of darkness.

Our one and only river, the Yamuna, has become a sewer fouled by human waste, chemical effluents and half-burnt bodies. People continue to bathe in it because their forefathers did so. We drink its water, filtered though it is, at our own peril. Those of us who can afford it, prefer bottled mineral water. What bothers us most is the foul air we have to inhale day and night. It gets fouler by the day as more buses, cars and scooters take to our already congested roads. I, who had not known illness in my long life, was stricken by viral flu. The fever left me but the cough persists. I know if I got out of the city for a few days, my chest and bronchial tubes would clear. I can't leave my place of work because I have to earn my living. The same holds true for all other citizens.

As citizens we have reason to be angry. Many of the things that make our cities unliveable can be taken care of: Put an immediate ban on emptying sewers and pouring effluents into our rivers. Declare at least one day in the week a day when petrol or diesel-run vehicles (except ambulances, fire brigades, and police cars) will not be allowed on the roads. No more sermons, speeches and learned papers on the subject. It is time for action. The time is now.

13 February 1999

Among the crawlers

A sentence used by L.K. Advani on the supine attitude of the Indian media during the Emergency will be quoted in history books because it sums up the gutlessness of our tribe of pen-pushers. He said, 'She (Mrs Gandhi) only asked you to bend, you decided to crawl.' He was right then; he would be right if he repeated the remark with regard to the media men of today. But let it not be forgotten that there were a few journals that closed down in protest, and many journalists were clapped into jail by the Emergency regime.

Others who protested mildly and pleaded for lifting of the Emergency and the release of political prisoners were spared in order to create the impression that the Government had not stamped out all criticism. the *Illustrated Weekly of India,* of which I was then editor, fell in this category of mild protesters (I supported the Emergency but opposed censorship of the press). Advani acknowledged this in his book published soon after the Emergency was lifted.

I have little doubt that if Emergency was imposed again, media reaction would be much the same as it was in the mid-1970s. A handful of media men would put down their pens in protest, a handful would be gaoled, the vast majority will bend backwards to toe the government line (crawl when only asked to bend). I will give an instance to prove my point.

A few weeks ago I was asked to preside over the launch of a book on corruption in Indian life. I was given only a couple of hours' notice, as the person who had agreed to do so had let the publishers down. I was down with fever and had not read the book. However, when I was told that L.K. Advani and V.P. Singh would be speaking, I agreed to go. I knew it would be my only chance to tell Advani to his face what I thought of him.

I thought very well of Advani as a clean, upright and able man. That is why I agreed to propose his name for elections to the Lok Sabha from New Delhi. I have every reason to believe that my doing so swung a substantial Sikh vote in Advani's favour. He won.

My disenchantment began when Advani started his *rath yatra* from Somnath to Ayodhya. I criticized his move then. I repeated my criticism at the book launch: 'You sowed the dragon's teeth which led to the destruction of the Babri Masjid,' I said. 'You are a clever coiner of words. You turned the Babri Masjid into a *dhaancha* and a disputed structure; your *parivar* parrots these expressions to this day. You denigrated critics like me as pseudo-secularists. Your brainless followers continue to use the same expression for people like me.'

I reassured Advani that I still held him in high regard as a man of honour and integrity. 'Two things I will never believe about you— that you feather your nest, or are unfaithful to your wife.' The remark amused Advani as well as the assemblage. So did the next one: 'You are a puritan. You do not drink, you do not smoke, you do not womanize.' And after a pause, 'Such men are dangerous.'

Needless to say, my hosts were acutely embarrassed by my speech. I wanted to get it off my chest, and I did. Advani did not seem to mind and said he would answer me at a more appropriate occasion than the launch of a book. Fair enough. What appalled me was the media reporting. Only one national daily gave my outburst the prominence it merited. All others blotted my name out of their reports. Most blatant was the coverage by Doordarshan. While all the other speakers were shown, the man presiding over the function was not. It was quite a feat of cinematography.

13 March 1999

Crime uncontrolled

You hear the same sort of stories from all parts of the country: it is not safe to go out after dark; it is not safe for old people to stay alone; housewives must not open doors to strangers even if they pretend to be postmen or come to check your electric meters; school-going children must be seen getting into the school bus or inside school gates lest they be abducted and held for ransom.

If big cities are unsafe, the countryside is no less so; in some places it's the Naxalites, at others armed gangs of landowners. Most politicians have armed musclemen of their own to contend with rival politicians with private armies of goondas. There are robberies on trains and buses.

There seems to be no dearth of firearms available without licences. Once acquired, there is a compulsive itch to use them at the slightest provocation. What has gone wrong with our countrymen? Do they want the country to dissolve into a chaos of violence?

'There is anger everywhere,' suggested a friend by way of explanation. 'Anger against whom?' I asked. 'Everyone,' she replied. 'The entire system. Otherwise, how can you explain boys throwing stones at passing trains, buses and cars, and running away? For no reason whatsoever, innocent people are killed. There is no follow-up. No arrests, no punishment.'

It is true. There is no respect for the law. How can there be any when our lawmakers take the law into their hands and bash each other up?—when a member who assaults a minister in a Legislative Assembly and is ordered to be arrested by the Speaker, is promptly let out on bail by a High Court? How can we expect better behaviour from common citizens?

C. Rajagopalachari used to say that religion is our best policeman. That may have been so during his time when religions had a social purpose and people were more religious. Now, religions have little social purpose, and the people practise their rites as matters of habit, without conviction. Another guardian of morality was the family. Erring offspring were brought to book by their parents and elders. Now, families have disintegrated; school teachers teach their pupils how to read and write but are no longer gurus to guide them on the path of rectitude, to tell them what is right and what is wrong.

When we have lost respect for our lawmakers and politicians, rulers and civil servants, judges and magistrates, and have less fear of the police, who can prevent us from venting our frustration and anger at everything we find around us? No matter whether we change our governments or impose President's rule on states at different times, defiance of law will continue unabated. It is indeed a very sorry state of affairs.

3 April 1999

A nation of windbags

The one thing India will never be short of is natural gas emanating from the mouths of our *netas*. What they lack in deeds, they make up for by indulging in long-winded orations. They are at their best pointing out the shortcomings of rivals and covering up their own. Real issues facing the country are bypassed as being of little consequence. This was clearly evident in the debate preceding the vote of confidence in the Vajpayee government.

The Government's failure to check pollution of the environment should have been highlighted by speakers of the Opposition parties. As it was, only one speaker alluded to the sorry state of the Ganga, the holiest of our many holy rivers. He talked of the filth, carcasses of animals and accumulation of scum along the ghats of Varanasi. You may recall that Rajiv Gandhi started his tenure as prime minister with the announcement that cleansing of the Ganga would be his first priority; that factories spilling effluents into the river would be closed down and throwing half-charred human corpses would be forbidden.

None of this has taken place. Not only has Ganga *jal* become unsafe to drink, even bathing in it has become a health hazard. It is the same with the Yamuna: human waste continues to flow into it as do industrial effluents. Hardly anything remains of our beloved Kalindi, as it was once known; it has become a sluggish, moving sewer. If you don't believe me, spend a few minutes at the Okhla barrage where the stretch of water had once made it Dilliwalas' favourite picnic spot. They have a yacht and a boat club there, but those who indulge in these pastimes have to stuff their nostrils with cotton wool against bad odour.

I have little doubt that the other rivers are in as poor a shape as the Ganga and the Yamuna and that the people living along the banks of the Narmada, Krishna, Tapti and Godavari are the same, having the same bad habits as those inhabiting the regions along the rivers of northern India.

Did you hear anyone talking about the Government's failure to check degradation of the land, deforestation, the silting of rivers and dams? Did you hear anyone talk of mounting illiteracy or poor health services? And of course no one dared to touch the most important issue of all: the urgent need to tackle the suicidal rate of increase in our population. They stick to levelling charges of corruption against each other, because there is plenty of incriminating material available on both sides for them to go so far and no further.

What the country needs are doers and not talkers. I am convinced that any government that takes bold steps in implementing what the country needs, however unpopular it may become at first, will win the respect and support of present and future generations.

1 May 1999

What a mess!

What an unholy mess we have made of our country! It is no use casting all the blame on politicians; we have to share the blame because we elected them. If they succeeded in fooling us, we were foolish enough to be taken in by their words. So we go in for yet another general election, the third in three years, and blow up another Rs 1,000 crore. Will the outcome be any different from the hodgepodge *khichree* of parties that we cooked up for the last Parliament? The post-election scenario may be much the same as it is today unless we analyse the weaknesses of the past coalition governments and eliminate the elements that brought about their downfall.

We know that there are many cases pending against Jayalalitha and that she indulged in arm-twisting the government to prevent them from being brought to a conclusion. Sonia Gandhi is in the same predicament. In the Bofors case, the accusing finger points towards her family. Like Jayalalitha, she does her best to avoid the truth about the kickbacks taken over the gun deal from being fully exposed. So any government which prosecutes the case with zeal has to be toppled. Thus Sitaram Kesri brought down the Gujral government. Before that Deve Gowda, Chandra Shekhar and V.P. Singh met the same fate. If charges of corruption pending against senior politicians including Laloo Prasad Yadav, Sukh Ram and a few others are speedily disposed of, their mischief potential will be vastly reduced.

The task of cleaning up the mess rests squarely in the hands of the electorate. Whatever its regional loyalties, it must look at national interests from a different perspective. The issues are fairly clear. It is Hindutva versus secularism; it is about giving high priority to family planning, preserving the environment, eradicating illiteracy, increasing agricultural and industrial output, reducing unemployment, controlling crime and corruption, avoiding wasteful expenditure on celebrations, and cutting down on holidays. If we do not address ourselves to these national issues, we will end up electing yet another Parliament without giving a single party or a combination of like-minded parties, a clear mandate to take the country forward. Ponder over this before you make up your mind whom to vote for.

Final warning

My youngest brother who owned among other things, a restaurant, kept late hours because he made it a point to stay on till closing time. He would often tell me 'K. Singh, of two things you can never be sure: one, when a person may drop in to have a meal, and two, when death will come to you.'

A *vaidji* whom I often visited in his shop while taking an after-dinner stroll, disagreed. He said death gives you many signals before it finally arrives to take you away. He narrated an anecdote about a wealthy man who became a friend of Yama, the messenger of death. One day he made a request to Yama, 'You and I have been close friends for many years. I ask you for just one favour: please give me timely warning that my time on earth will soon be over so that I can arrange my worldly affairs before I go.' Yama agreed to do so. However, one day the wealthy man died suddenly leaving his business in a mess. When he met Yama, he complained bitterly of having been let down by him. 'Not at all,' protested Yama, 'instead of one warning, I gave you several. First, I made your hair turn grey. Then I deprived you of your teeth; then I made you hard of hearing and vision. Finally, I made you feeble of mind. If you still ignored these warnings, you have only yourself to blame.'

It is true that an enfeebled mind is, as it were, the final alarm bell for the start of the long march towards the unknown. A mindless existence is like being dead while breathing.

We begin to think of death only in our old age. In our young years time hangs heavy and we delude ourselves into believing it will go on for ever and ever.

8 May 1999

Sonia: *Bahu* not *beti*

As far as I am concerned, whether she was born in Turin or Tuticorin should be of little consequence. She is a better Indian than Sharad Pawar, Sangma, Tariq Anwar or I, because while she *chose* to become Indian, we are Indians by accident of birth. I am sure if we had had any say in the matter, most, if not all of us, would have preferred to have been born in countries more prosperous and peaceful than ours. Consequently, this patriotic chest-thumping about being Indian-born and therefore fitter to lead the country, is arrant nonsense.

My reservations about Sonia Gandhi arise from statements she made at different times in the past about entering Indian politics. To start with, she kept her options open for many years after she had married Rajiv Gandhi. She made no secret of her distaste for politicians and threatened to divorce her husband and quit India if he joined politics. He shared her views and kept his distance from people who surrounded his mother, Indira Gandhi and younger brother Sanjay. The couple was extremely upset when Mrs Gandhi imposed Emergency on the country; and when she was humiliated in the polls after Emergency was lifted, they seriously contemplated leaving India. Their plans changed when Sanjay, who hogged the political scene, was killed in a plane crash.

Rajiv filled the vacuum created by his brother's death. Sonia became a dutiful and the favourite *bahu* of the prime minister. It was at this stage that she decided to accept Indian nationality. The assassination of her mother-in-law and her husband would have ended the hegemony of the Nehru-Gandhi dynasty if Sonia had not agreed to assume the mantle. She became the icon of the Congress party. The Opposition, which disliked the dynasty, was nevertheless eager to exploit the warm feelings the masses have towards the family: they put up the other *bahu*, Maneka Gandhi, as their anti-Sonia ballistic missile. It is common knowledge that Mrs Gandhi disliked Maneka and threw her out of the house. Parties opposed to the Congress hated Mrs Gandhi and decided that if the Congress could have Sonia as an icon, Maneka would be theirs.

Since all is fair in the dirty game of Indian politics, I can understand why super patriots who stand for everything *swadeshi* from womb to tomb, should make an issue of Sonia having been born in Italy. But it is difficult to see Messrs Pawar, Sangma and Anwar toe the same line. Pawar has a history of ditching his leaders. Having exploited Sonia's popularity and seeing new life in the Congress, I am not surprised at his gambling for the top post by doing the dirty on her. Sangma joining him leaves me baffled. Tariq Anwar does not count for very much.

29 May 1999

Men are brainier

Girls do better than boys; men do better than women. That sums up the performance of males and females in their lives. Year after year we learn from the results of the final school-leaving examinations, that girls outshine boys. The simple explanation is that school girls do not waste as much time as boys on playing fields. In college, sports are not compulsory; so boys spend more time poring over textbooks and less in kicking footballs about or playing cricket. By then, most girls' minds are preoccupied with thoughts of marriage. Their level of performance in examinations drops while the performance of boys picks up. They end their college years almost at par. This is evident in the results of the combined civil service examinations. Although some girls are occasionally among the top ten, the proportion of boys who succeed is much higher than that of the girls.

By their mid-twenties, girls become women, boys become men. Women begin to fall behind as achievers, men forge ahead in every field: science, engineering, medicine, arts, literature, music, commerce, industry, law, politics—just about everything including activities which are considered women's domains like cooking and stitching clothes. (Have you ever heard of a woman head chef of a hotel or a woman master tailor?) When women rise to the top in their professions, they are looked upon as specimens as rare as albino tigers.

There is more to male predominance as achievers than women having to perform household chores and looking after children. It would seem that male superiority is designed by nature. In the recent issue of the *Journal of Human Evolution,* scientists have been able to establish that males of all species have bigger brains than females. They started with examining eighty-three rhesus monkeys (higher primates which possess similar patterns of mental and sexual development as humans). The leader of the team of scientists, Dean Falk, asserts that while it had previously been assumed that male brains are bigger because their bodies are bigger, this is not true. 'Eighty-eight per cent of the difference is attributable to sex rather than body size.'

Falk's study further shows that female brains grow to adult size at 3.57 years; male brains attain full size at 6.08 years. Dr Falk believes that men outperform women in all fields because of the difference in the sizes of their brains. Dean Falk is a woman.

12 June 1999

Loving one's neighbour

Now that we have overcome our phobia of losing to Pakistan in cricket, Kargil has become our national obsession. It disturbs our nights' sleep and our moon's repose. As bodies of our jawans and officers who fell on the battlefield are flown in for burial or cremation, the distance between us and our not-too-friendly neighbour Pakistan increases. If a little pimple erupts on our small toe, pain wracks our bodies and we remain restless till it's removed. Kargil is not a little pimple on our little toe; it is a big bump on our foreheads which throbs with pain. We cannot think about anything else except Kargil; we do not talk about anything except Kargil. We cannot wish it away. We ask ourselves: 'Is this the way a country should behave towards its neighbour?'

The paradox is that we are and we are not at war with Pakistan. We describe it as 'a war situation' (whatever that means). However, two things are clear and incontrovertible: one, that the fighting is taking place entirely on our territory and not a single bullet has been fired in Pakistan; two, the men who are fighting us are not Indian nationals but aliens who sneaked into our territory through Pakistan either with its knowledge or connivance. Pakistan owes India and other nations of the world an explanation as to why it allowed this situation to develop. If Pakistan means to cultivate good neighbourly relations with us, it must help us to get rid of these intruders. Knowing the internal pressures under which the Pakistan government functions, this is asking for the impossible.

While we must not rest till the last intruder has been expelled or slain, we should not let war hysteria overtake us. We were caught napping in Kargil; we must not be caught napping again. Nor peevishly indulge in actions which could be construed by Pakistan as hostile. The decision to undertake naval exercises in the Arabian Sea rather than the usual Bay of Bengal is one such unwise act. It might have been wiser to invite the Pakistani navy to conduct joint exercises with ours, and so allay their fears. We are the bigger and more powerful neighbour; we should teach Pakistan how neighbours should behave towards each other.

19 June 1999

Sweat and blood

There is a Chinese proverb, 'If you sweat more in times of peace you lose less blood in times of war.' They taught us this lesson in 1962. The Pakistanis are teaching us the same lesson again in 1999. In 1962, the Chinese occupied many areas we claimed were ours. They laid roads in this area and stationed their troops. It was after many months that we discovered their armed presence in our territory. We raised a hue and cry around the world. Our leaders, mainly Nehru and Krishna Menon, made war-like speeches about 'vacating aggression' and driving the Chinese intruders out. Nobody believed us: 'If it was your territory, how is it you knew nothing about the Chinese being in it?' they asked.

The Chinese gave us a bloody punch in the nose. Our noses bled because the Chinese had sweated in times of peace to prepare for war. We did not, and lost face.

The scenario is repeating itself. We never had any illusions about Pakistan's intentions towards us. We should have watched every move they made and countered it promptly. We did not. While we were napping, they stealthily occupied many strategic points in our territory, fortified them and stocked them with arms, ammunition and rations to last them for many months. Now we are having to pay a heavy price in blood to get them out. However, let us make it clear to them that no matter what it costs us in terms of human lives and money, drive them out we will—to their last man on our soil.

How long will it last? We get conflicting accounts. We are told the intruders are being pushed out; they are running out of ammunition, food and water. In the same breath we are told to be prepared for a long action lasting till the onset of winter. If the latter is more likely than a quick end to the confrontation, then we must put aside our preoccupations which detract our attention from the important task of driving out hostile elements from our soil.

The pending general elections is going to be a major distraction. If action does not end till mid-July, it would be sensible to postpone it by a Presidential Ordinance or an Act of Parliament, but with the clear understanding that a national government comprising all the leading parties will replace the present one with Atal Behari Vajpayee still at its helm, and George Fernandes continuing as the defence minister—the façade of continuity must be maintained. It would be ideal if Sonia Gandhi could be persuaded to accept the deputy prime ministership and thereafter induct men like Manmohan Singh, Sharad Pawar, Sangma, any one—Communist, Akali, Samajwadi, Bahujan Samaj, DMK or AIADMK.

A truly national government would send a message to Pakistan and the rest of the world that when our frontiers are threatened, we stand together as one people.

Garbage called astrology

I do not think we Indians will ever get out of the clutches of astrologers, palmists, numerologists and other charlatans who live by making forecasts. It is clear as daylight that planets do not influence human behaviour in any way, and all that is attributed to people according to the signs of the zodiac is absolute hogwash. In 1962, when eight planets were in conjunction *(ashtagraha)* and every single astrologer pronounced that the end of the world had come, nothing happened. The planets were in similar conjunction earlier this year.

This time, soothsayers did not predict doomsday and were saved from being proved wrong again. But no matter how wrong they are proved over and over again, our gullibility is such that we continue to repose faith in their predictions. Every newspaper and magazine has its paid astrologer. Readers pore over their predictions day after day, hoping for a windfall in their fortunes or in dread of an imminent catastrophe. Nothing happens. Nevertheless we continue to call astrology a science which it most certainly is not. We have become mentally sick.

The prime time for the tribe of forecasters is the eve of elections. They make a killing predicting who will win and which party will lose. Our widely circulated magazines like *India Today, Sunday* and the *Week* have already launched this exercise. The only exception so far is *Outlook*. The *Asian Age* has gone ahead with publishing on its front page, other items from the astrologers' lexicon: *Rahukal, Yamagand, Gulikakal.* If we take this kind of rubbish in our daily diet, how can we hope to cultivate a scientific temper?

I have been provoked into writing this angry piece by a homeopath (I refrain from naming him as it might damage his practice) who besides doling out sugar-coated pills, also indulges in astrology. He sent me his manuscript with a request that I write the foreword. I begged to be excused as I did not have the time to read what he had written. He wrote back an angry letter telling me that in his book he had predicted six months ago that India would make it to the finals of the World Cup cricket tournament. And if that proved to be wrong, I could dump his manuscript in the waste-paper basket. I wrote back on his own letter, 'How can all educated men like you believe in this kind of medieval garbage?' That very day, our team went out of the reckoning in the tournament. The learned doctor's manuscript was not dumped in the waste-paper basket but sold to the *kabariwala,* as all books on astrology deserve to be.

26 June 1999

Turbulent weather

The flight from Delhi to Calcutta was as smooth as can be expected during the monsoons.

It was only after the descent on the Netaji Subhas Chandra Bose airport that the plane began to run into turbulent weather and the 'fasten seat belts' order was flashed on the panels above the seats. The plane began to rock violently. There were continuous flashes of lightning, some very close to the aircraft. As the order came for the crew to be seated in preparation for landing, the plane flew out of the black clouds and we could see the vast spread of glittering lights of Calcutta (Kolkata, the capital of Paschim Banga) beneath us; they looked as if all the stars in the heavens had come down on the earth to welcome us. The plane made a very smooth landing.

This is the kind of turbulent weather our country is going through right now. We have to fasten our seat belts and not be unduly alarmed by the plane's rocking or by the dark clouds, lightning and thunder. We have to reaffirm our faith in the competence and determination of our jawans to drive out the intruders who have sneaked into our land. At the same time, we should send a message to the people of Pakistan that we bear no ill-will towards them. It is their government, and more than their government, their army that has betrayed them and us by colluding with religious fanatics and mercenaries to encroach upon our territory. No nation worth its salt will tolerate *goondagardi* on its soil. Nor will India. No matter what it costs us in terms of human lives or money, we will not rest till the last intruder has either departed, or is dead. We have been wronged. Nations of the world are agreed that we have been wronged by the rulers of Pakistan. We will rectify the wrong done to us by mustering up all resources at our command.

Having failed to prove its innocence to the United States, the European nations and even to its old ally China, Pakistan's rulers are trying to whip up sympathy for themselves from among Muslim nations. It may gain some support from states that have an unthinking knee-jerk response to every confrontation between a Muslim and non-Muslim country, but this is not likely to yield very much support even from their co-religionists. A jehad has to be for a just cause, not for the purpose of blatant aggression. And blatant aggression is exactly what the Pakistani rulers have allowed to be committed against India.

10 July 1999

Daghaa (Betrayal)

It is becoming increasingly difficult to believe words spoken by Pakistani leaders. Our faith in their integrity has been rudely shaken. After fifty years of acceptance of the Line of Control as the border between the two countries, what provoked them to allow elements hostile to India to cross it and entrench themselves in our temporarily unoccupied outposts? And now Pakistan's Prime Minister Nawaz Sharif, having realized that military adventurism has turned world opinion against Pakistan, is desperately trying to wriggle out of the trap he laid for himself and his country.

First he denied that Pakistan had any hand in the intruders getting a foothold on Indian territory. He was confronted with hard evidence proving Pakistan's collusion in the sneak operation. Then he denied that regulars of the Pakistani army were in any way involved in the operation. He has now received concrete evidence in the Pakistani soldiers captured or killed on the Indian side of the Line of Control. All options of lying his way out of the predicament have closed.

If he now orders the unconditional withdrawal of intruders from Indian territory, he will have to face the ire of the hawks in his armed forces and the fundamentalist political groups in his country who are forever clamouring for jehad against India. I would not take a month's insurance on the life of hapless Nawaz Sharif. He has betrayed us and he has betrayed his own countrymen.

I have little doubt that 'Operation Vijay' will end in victory for India. *'Nasr min Allah Fateh-un qareeb'* (Allah grants victory to people whose cause is just), said Prophet Mohammed. Our cause is just; Pakistan's is not: it has allowed its leaders to commit *daghaa* against us.

17 July 1999

After the war

In the expectation that by the time this piece appears in print, the last infiltrator will have departed from our side of the Line of Control in Kargil and guns from either side will have fallen silent, we should ask ourselves: 'What should we do next?'

In the recent conflict, young men laid down their lives to protect their motherland and gave whatever they could afford to help families who lost their sons. However, we must remind ourselves that we should not need disputes with our neighbours in order to put up a united front. By now it should have become an integral part of our national character.

The need to mend fences with Pakistan has become imperative. The conflict poisoned the atmosphere in both countries. This must be dissipated—the sooner the better. Those of us who have friends in Pakistan should assure them that we bear them no ill-will. On the contrary, we have always been eager to be on brotherly terms with them and should reaffirm our resolve to resume the friendly relations that existed between us before Kargil exploded in our faces.

It will not be easy, but the process should be set in motion at once. Visas should be given to visitors without delay; cross-border buses, trains and other services be resumed; Pakistani artists, scholars and poets be welcomed in India; Indian artists, scholars and poets be welcomed in Pakistan. And people of both countries should swear by whatever they hold most sacred, that never again will they allow suspicion and hatred to steal into their minds.

24 July 1999

Views from the other side

I have a lot of friends in Pakistan who do not toe the government line but have minds of their own. I was unable to communicate with them while the Kargil war was on. But as soon as the guns fell silent, I sought them out to find out what the Pakistanis in the streets of Karachi, Lahore and Islamabad made of the fiasco. Did they accept the fact that every drop of blood that was shed in the confrontation between us and them was shed on Indian soil? Did they know that the men who were killed on their side were not only *mujahideens* as it was first put out, but regular soldiers of the Pak army, and India had provided concrete evidence including bodies of their dead and documents found on them to prove it?

A lady who lives in Karachi and came to call on me, admitted that their official media and sections of the anti-India press had done its best to obfuscate the issue by harping on the larger question of the future of Kashmir, and accusing India of harbouring ill-will against Pakistan. But she added that Pakistanis are not as angry with India as they are with Nawaz Sharif for allowing the Indians to humiliate them once again on the battlefield. Pakistanis have not forgotten their disastrous defeat in the 1971 war. They were hoping that their army would level the score by giving the Indians a bloody punch on their noses. It did not turn out that way. 'They must hate our guts,' I suggested. She paused before she replied, 'Hate is too strong a word. Let me just say that they do not have much love for the Indians. Victors can afford to be forgiving towards the vanquished; the vanquished find it much harder to forgive victors.'

She went on to explain the changing scenario in Pakistan. Religious fundamentalism is rapidly gaining ground. You see a resurgence of rituals in homes; and the younger generation of even westernized Pakistanis use Islamic terminology these days. More and more women are wearing burkhas of the Iranian style. 'I find this more alarming than hostility towards India,' she said. And for good measure, added, 'I also notice growing religious intolerance in India. Travelling in buses and trains where people don't recognize me as a Pakistani, I hear a lot of nasty things being said not only about Pakistan, but about Muslims.'

Among the Marwaris

The stereotype image of a Marwari is a skinflint who starts off with nothing besides his *lota,* a few paise tied in a knot of his *dhoti,* and a few years later, becomes a millionaire. At school we used to sing a doggerel which went somewhat as follows: *'Marwar no baanio, Mumbai seher ma aaiyo* and lived on two pice of *ghee* and *atta.'* They are also known to be close-fisted and calculating. They never give away anything unless they are sure they can get it back with compound interest.

Having worked for a Marwari (K.K. Birla) and befriended some others, notably his niece, Manjushri Khaitan and her parents (Mr and Mrs B.K. Birla), I can vouch for the fact that I have yet to meet people of that class of affluence more courteous and uncalculating in their generosity than they. To meet the upper crust of Marwaris, rather than going to Mumbai *seher,* one should go to the capital city of Paschim Banga, Kolkata. That's exactly what I did a few weeks ago.

It was monsoon time. Dark clouds spread across the sky. By the time Col. Ramesh Dadlani (who works with K.K. Khemka, an associate of B.K. Birla) came to take me out for lunch, a strong wind had picked up. Ramesh is a very dapperly-dressed Punjabi. During his last posting in Calcutta, he fell in love with the city and decided to make it his home. He took premature retirement, joined Khemka, and has been with the firm ever since. I asked him what working for Marwaris was like. 'They are good employers,' he replied, 'very courteous, and generous. If you do the work assigned to you, they treat you like a member of the family.'

I asked him why there was no resentment among Bengalis against them. He replied, 'They (the Marwaris) do not throw their weight about or flaunt their wealth. They have put down their roots in Calcutta and give liberally to local charities like schools, colleges, hospitals and temples. Upper-class Bengalis are snobs, and for many years they would not take Marwaris into their swanky clubs. So Marwaris, being captains of industry, joined the Rotary movement. You will notice their predominant presence in Rotary Clubs. They never rub Bengalis the wrong way.' That is true.

Only a week before my visit, a brash young Marwari had the audacity to use the word 'Bongs' for Bengalis on his website. Bengalis exploded with anger. My friend Sunil Gangopadhyay, Bengal's leading novelist, who did not think it mattered if he used the Sikh stereotype to portray a villain in one of his novels, blasted the Marwari and went ahead to proclaim that Calcutta would soon be Kolkata, and West Bengal, Paschim Banga. So be it.

At Khemka's luncheon party at Hotel
Hindustan International where I often stayed
in the past, of the over-two-dozen guests, all
but four were Marwaris. Among the prominent
ones were S. Bangla (tea), Bangur (chemicals
and electrical appliances), Daga (automobile
parts and electric components), Jaiswal
(hotels), Jalan (theatre), Kanoria (chemicals),
Khaitan (fans), Jhunjhunwala (silks, ice-cream
and leather), Kejriwal (tea), Khemka (railway
components), Rohatgi (automobile parts),
Sureka (real estate), Rajgarhia (steel) and
Sadhu (paper).

I noticed only four non-Marwaris—Jit
Paul—Swaraj Paul's brother (hotels, tea, real
estate), P.K. Sen (tea), A. Aikat (TV) and
Harbhajan Singh (Allahabad Bank). Marwari
predominance in the business and social life
of Calcutta was even more evident at the
Rotary Club dinner meeting at Grand Hotel
where K.K. Khemka was sworn in as the new
president. Among the 200-odd guests present,
barely two dozen were non-Marwaris. Of
them, three were my guests—Vice-Chancellor
Surabhi Banerjee, her husband and daughter.
It spoke well of both communities: of the

Bengalis, for their spirit of accommodation of so many outsiders who were doing better in life than they.

7 August 1999

Prepare for death while alive

I do not know when I was born, because in my village, no records of births or deaths were maintained. And in my part of western Punjab, no one bothered with such things as horoscopes. My father was away in Delhi; my mother, who was barely literate, did not think birthdays were of any importance. My year of birth was put down later as 1915—it could as well have been 1914 or 1916—and my father put down February 2 as my date of birth. His mother, who was there when I was born, told me later that her son had got it all wrong and that I was born in mid-August. So I am right in saying that I am not sure when I was born. And I cannot say when I will die except that it will not be too long from now. By any reckoning I am eighty-five years old, give or take a year.

Humra Qureshi had come to interview me on what she assumed was my eighty-fifth birthday, for a column she writes for the *Times of India*. After putting me through the usual routine of questions about my past and present, she came to the final 'What now?' I did not give a very coherent answer on what I planned to do in the years left to me. However, after she left I pondered over the matter for a long time. Socrates had advised, 'Always be occupied in the practice of dying.' How does one practice dying? The Dalai Lama, then only fifty-eight, advised meditating on it. I am not sure how thinking about it can help. It is particularly difficult for someone like me who has rejected belief in God and the possibility of another life after death, be it reincarnation or the Day of Judgement followed by heaven or hell. However, there comes a time when one stops regarding death as something that comes to other people with the realization that you too are on the waiting list. If you are taken ill, you begin to think about it sooner than if you are in good physical shape. In either case, by the time you are in your eighties, it begins to preoccupy your mind more and more. You think of what

you could have done in your life but failed to
do. You wanted to become a millionaire but
did not go beyond accumulating a modest
bank balance; you wanted to become prime
minister of India, a champion tennis player,
cricketer, golfer, athlete etc., but did not get
beyond being part of the second eleven of your
college team or a mediocre club player. Or, in
my case, I wanted to win many literary awards,
earn huge royalties but ended up as a second-
rate book writer who would be forgotten a few
years after he was gone. So the first thing to
get over through meditation or just pondering,
is the feeling of regret over your failures—you
did your best but it was not good enough to get
you to the top. So what?

Equally important is to get over the sense of
guilt for having wronged other people. Everyone
of us causes hurt to someone or the other in our
lives. This rankles in our minds. It is advisable
to make amends by expressing regret. Having
peace of mind should be a person's top priority
in the final years of his life. Prayers, pilgrimages
and religious rituals are not as effective as candid
confession and seeking forgiveness. There also
comes a time when you begin to regard your

body as no more than something which encases your real self, like an envelope that contains a letter with a vital message. The body will perish when the envelope is torn open; will anything survive after the body is gone? Will the letter inside the torn envelope be something worth reading after the envelope ceases to exist? I do not have answers to these questions, and none of the answers given by people who believe that something of us survives after death, makes sense to me.

All I hope for is that when death comes to me, it comes swiftly, without much pain; like fading away in sound slumber. Till that time I will strive to live as full a life as I did in my younger days. My inspirations are Dylan Thomas's immortal lines:

Do not go gentle into that good night,
Old age should burn and rave at close of
day;
Rage, rage against the dying of the light.

One should prepare oneself to die like a man; no moaning, groaning or crying for reprieve. Allama Iqbal put it beautifully:

Nishaan-e-mard-e-Momin ba to goyam?
Choon margaayad, tabassum bar lab-e-ost

(You ask me for signs of a man of faith?
When death comes to him, he has a smile
on his lips.)

21 August 1999

Independence Day

Our century's final Independence Day will be
different from others we have celebrated so
far. This time last year, not many would have
taken a bet on Atal Behari Vajpayee unfolding
the tricolour and addressing the nation from
the ramparts of the Red Fort once again. But
there he is, and with more than a fair chance
of being there yet again. Though he heads a
makeshift government *(kaam chalao sarkar),*
his speech is not likely to be *kaam chalao.*
He is undoubtedly one of the best orators we
have heard on similar occasions. And though
he is wise enough to know that he must not
make his oration an electioneering harangue to

attack rival political parties or indulge in chest-thumping over his government's achievements, he will inevitably (though subtly) dwell on the inadequacies of the other aspirants for power, and paint a rosy picture of his dreams for the future of the country.

Our relations with our neighbour, Pakistan, have never been icier than they are today. They will remain frozen as long as Pakistani-backed militants continue to be active in Kashmir and the border districts of Himachal. How will he break the ice and the impasse? Clearly he will have to do more than take a bus ride to Lahore. The onus of resolving the Kashmir problem rests entirely on the shoulders of the Kashmiris. It is they who must come up with proposals which are practicable and acceptable to both India and Pakistan. Kashmir has soured our relations ever since we became independent nations. Much blood and vast sums of money have been wasted trying to settle the issue by use of force. We have to go beyond reiterating our respective positions ad nauseum and reach a settlement acceptable to the three parties: the people of Jammu and Kashmir, India and Pakistan.

Meanwhile, more important problems which have been put on the back-burner for too long because of our preoccupations with our neighbour, internecine political wranglings and frequent elections, must be brought to the forefront. For the hundredth time, I repeat: 'Please Mr or Mrs Prime Minister-to-be, make family planning compulsory, make felling trees and fouling the environment crimes punishable by heavy fines and imprisonment. Otherwise you will be held guilty of letting down our country.'

The one and only Nirad Babu

'There is nothing more dreadful to an author than neglect, compared with which reproach, hatred and opposition are names of happiness.' These words of Dr Johnson were inscribed by Nirad Chaudhuri on my copy of his book, *A Passage to England*. These words hold the key to Nirad's past life and present personality. They explain the years of neglect of one who must have at all times been a most remarkable man; his attempt to attract attention by cocking-the-snook at people who had neglected him; and the 'reproach, hatred and opposition' that he succeeded in arousing as a result of his rudeness.

Nirad had been writing in Bengali for many years. But it was not until the publication of his first book in English, *The Autobiography of an Unknown Indian,* that he really aroused the interest of the class to which he belonged and which, because of the years of indifference to him, he had come heartily to loathe—the Anglicized upper-middle class of India. He did this with calculated contempt. He knew that the wogs were more English than Indian, but were fond of proclaiming their patriotism at the expense of the British. That having lost their own traditions and not having fully imbibed those of England, they were a breed with pretensions to intellectualism that seldom went beyond reading the blurbs and reviews of books.

He therefore decided to dedicate the work 'To the British Empire'. The wogs took the bait, and having only read the dedication, sent up a howl of protest. Many people who would not have otherwise read the autobiography, discovered to their surprise that there was nothing anti-Indian in its pages. On the contrary, it was the most beautiful picture of eastern Bengal that anyone had ever painted. And at long last, India had produced a writer who did not cash in on naïve Indianisms but could write the English language as it should be written—and as few, if any, living Englishmen could write.

Nobody could afford to ignore Nirad Chaudhuri any more. He and his wife Amiya became the most sought-after couple in Delhi's upper-class circles. Anecdotes of his vast fund of knowledge were favourite topics at dinner parties.

The first story I heard of the Chaudhuri family was of a cocktail party hosted by the late Director-General of All India Radio, Colonel Lakshmanan. Nirad had brought his wife and sons (in shorts and full boots) to the function. After the introductions, the host asked what Nirad would like to drink, and mentioned that he had some excellent sherry.

'What kind of sherry?' asked the chief guest. Colonel Lakshmanan had, like most people, heard of only two kinds. 'Both kinds,' he replied. 'Do you like dry or sweet?' This wasn't good enough for Nirad, so he asked one of his sons to taste it and tell him. The thirteen-year-old lad took a sip, rolled it about his tongue, and after a thoughtful pause replied, 'Must be an Oloroso 1947'.

Nirad Babu could talk about any subject under the sun. There was not a bird, tree, butterfly or insect whose name he did not know in Latin, Sanskrit, Hindi and Bengali. Long before he left for London, he not only knew where the important monuments and museums were, but also the location of many famous restaurants. I heard him contradict a lady who had lived six years in Rome about the name of a street leading off from the Colosseum—and prove his contention. I've heard him discuss stars with astronomers, recite lines from an obscure fifteenth century French literature and advise a wine dealer on the best vintages from Burgundy. At a small function in honour of Laxness, the Icelandic winner of the Nobel Prize for literature, I heard Nirad lecture him on Icelandic literature.

Nirad was a small, frail man, little over five feet. He led a double life. At home he dressed in *dhoti-kurta* and sat on the floor to do his reading and writing. When leaving for work, he wore European dress: coat, tie, trousers and a monstrous khaki sola topi. As soon as he stepped out, street urchins would chant 'Johnnie Walker, left, right, left, right'.

Nirad Babu was not a modest man; he had great reason to be immodest. No Indian, living or dead, wrote the English language as well as he did. He was also a very angry man. When he was dismissed from service by a singularly half-baked I&B minister, Dr B.V. Keskar, he exploded with wrath. Years later, the Government of India wanted him to do a definitive booklet on the plight of the Hindu minority in East Pakistan and offered him a blank cheque for his services. Nirad, who was in dire financial straits, turned it down with contempt. 'The Government may have lifted its ban on Nirad Chaudhuri, but Nirad Chaudhuri has not lifted his ban on the Government of India,' he said to me when I conveyed Finance Minister T.T. Krishnamachari's proposal to him.

Chaudhuri's second book, *A Passage to England,* received the most glorious reviews in the English press. Three editions were rapidly sold out and it had the distinction of becoming the first book by an Indian author to have become a bestseller in England. The bay windows of London's famous bookshop, Foyles, were decorated with large-sized photographs of Nirad. Some Indian critics were, as in the past, extremely hostile. Nirad's reaction followed the same pattern. At first he tried not to be bothered by people 'who didn't know better', then burst with invective against the 'yapping curs'. I asked him how he reconciled himself to these two attitudes. After a pause he replied, 'When people say nasty things about my books without really understanding what I have written, I feel like a father who sees a drunkard make an obscene pass at his daughter. I want to chastise him.' Then, with a typically Bengali gesture demonstrating the form of chastisement, 'I want to give them a shoe-beating with my *chappal*.'

A few years ago Nirad Babu wrote an article for a prestigious London weekly in which he mentioned how hard he was finding life in Oxford, living on his royalties from books. I published extracts from it in my column. K.K. Birla wrote to me to tell Nirad Babu that he would be happy to give him a stipend for life for any amount in any currency he wanted. I forwarded Birla's letter to Nirad. He wrote back asking me to thank Birla for his generous offer, but refused to accept it. It is a pity that he accepted a CBE (Commander of the British Empire) from the British Government. He deserved a peerage, because he was in fact, a peerless man of intellect and letters.

14 August 1999

And now, the verdict

At election time, aspiring candidates make tall claims about their achievements. Their party spokesmen speak in even louder languages reminiscent of all-in wrestlers as they strut about the ring. Braying and bragging comes down to a lower pitch when votes are cast. Then we await the verdict of the electorate with bated breath. Thereafter, it is victory processions for the victorious; post-mortems for the vanquished—all blaming their closest party members for stabbing them in the back.

This has become the familiar pattern of our elections.

However, no matter what the outcome, there will be a decisive change in India's political scene. If the BJP and its allies manage to come out on top, they will have to rein in the extremist Hindu fundamentalists in their ranks. There should be no more talk of breaking mosques and building mandirs on their ruins. There should be no more talk of depriving Kashmir of its special status, or meddling with Muslim personal law. If they do, they will have a short lease in office.

The future of the Congress is more difficult to forecast. If Sonia Gandhi wins both her seats, her future as leader of the party and the continuing domination of the Nehru-Gandhi family will be assured for decades to come. If she loses both, it will be the end of her political ambitions, and a serious setback to the aspirations of her family. If she wins one and loses the other, the chances are that leaders of the breakaway group led by Sharad Pawar will reassert its right to control the party's future. I do not see the Communists loosening their grip in the states they have ruled, nor the regional parties in the north-east and the southern states diminishing in importance. On the surface, not very much will change.

I approve of the BJP's intention to introduce legislation which will prevent people from filing nominations in more than one constituency and make the tenure of the Lok Sabha a full period of five years. But I am not sure how they will be able to do so unless they have a decisive majority in both houses of Parliament. This is most unlikely. What they could and can do is to bring the innumerable cases of corruption and inciting violence against political leaders to speedy ends. Crooked politicians have mastered the art of procrastinating proceedings for years. If the new government means to start with a clean image, this should be its top priority.

4 September 1999

Unholy war against India

How seriously should we take Osama bin Laden's declaration of jehad against the US,

Russia and India? The Taliban, though they claim they have nothing to do with Osama, have been carrying on an undeclared jehad against us. They are evidently not concerned with the reactions of non-Muslims whom they have chosen as targets for their jehad, nor of the Muslims who live amongst us. Of course we will not take their threats lying down and give them as good as we get. But how will our Muslim brethren overcome the embarrassment caused to them? Above all, don't they realize that while posing as jehadis, they do grave disservice to Islam? As it is, a large section of non-Muslims believe that Muslims are fanatics unresponsive to reason and the changing world. Osama and the Taliban confirm this inaccurate and uncharitable view of Islam and the Muslims.

I have always maintained that the worst enemies of any religious community are bigots who assume the role of purveyors (*thekedaars*) of its religion: they pretend to be all-knowing and are ever eager to take up cudgels. The Sikhs had their Bhindranwale, the Hindus have their Vishwa Hindu Parishad, Shiv Sainiks and Bajrangdalis and Muslims have their

Mullahs, Talibans and jehadis. They make life miserable. They are not a new phenomenon. Our forefathers had to suffer the likes of them in their times. Prince Dara Shikoh (1615-54) wrote:

> *Paradise is where no Mullah resides*
> *May no one pay heed to his fatwas;*
> *In a street where a Mullah resides,*
> *No wise man is ever found.*

The history of India would have been different if Dara Shikoh had succeeded Shah Jehan as emperor rather than the bigot Aurangzeb who alienated his non-Muslim subjects and sowed the seeds of destruction of the Mughal dynasty. Likewise, Maharaja Ranjit Singh had harsh things to say about the Akalis: he described them as people with closed minds and lacking in vision. He used them in his battles against the *ghazis* who declared holy war against his kingdom. They fought with Ranjit's Muslim militia and repulsed the jehadis.

The Islamic world is going through a period of grave uncertainty. Within their ranks are fundamentalists like the Muslim brotherhood in Egypt and its counterparts in other Islamic countries. They are active in other Islamic countries recently liberated from Soviet domination. And they are trying to create trouble in the Muslim regions in China. It is the duty of Muslims to rid themselves of Bin Laden and the Talibans.

Mumbai's Star Achievers

In Mumbai more than anywhere else in India, nothing matters more than success. On top of its list of achievers are film stars. They are easy on the eyes, they are rich and make pots of money which elude sleuths of the income tax department. Next come industrialists who make a lot more money than film stars. They are usually pot-bellied and heavy-jowled by the time they become billionaires, and arouse the admiration-cum-envy of their fellow citizens. Musicians, painters and journalists come last in Mumbai's list of achievers.

This was very evident at the Giants International evening and award-giving ceremony. The organization was set up by

Nana Chudasama in 1972. It started giving awards in 1985. This year, the most sought-after by photographers, film cameramen and autograph-hunters, were Juhi Chawla and Salman Khan followed closely by Mukesh Ambani and Mahesh Bhupati. Last came Dr K. Ramamoorthy of Bombay Hospital, Rakhee Sapru of Cancer Patients Aid Association and Varghese Kurien.

Presiding over the function was Field Marshal Sam Maneckshaw. With the years he has become somewhat of a caricature of a Colonel Blimp. He takes credit for winning the war of the liberation of Bangladesh. He speaks very well but does not realize that it ill behoves a man of wisdom to use his tongue in praise of himself. The award-giving function and the dinner that followed, went on till midnight.

The next morning I got talking to my host Tarlochan Singh Sahney about the decline of Bombay from being the best administrated city of India to becoming a heavily congested, chaotic and goonda-ridden metropolis. I told him of Pinki Virani's book *Once Was Bombay* in which she puts the blame squarely on three men: M.A. Jinnah for making Bombay Muslims a people apart from Bombay's non-Muslims, L.K. Advani for his Somnath-Ayodhya *rath yatra* which led to the demolition of the Babri masjid followed by violence in Bombay, and Bal Thackeray whose Shiv Sainiks played the leading role in destroying the mosque and the slaughter of Bombay Muslims.

'Does she say nothing about the role of Morarji Desai?' Tarlochan asked me. I was surprised by his question as I regard Morarji as an honest politician, above communal prejudice, but somewhat narrow in his vision. 'Morarji Desai,' explained Tarlochan, 'introduced prohibition. Immediately, illicit hooch sprang up all over the state with the police in cahoots with the hooch-makers. Then he imposed a ban on gold import. And smuggling gold became a lucrative business. With these measures he created a nexus between law-breakers and law-keepers (the police). Between them they have corrupted the civic life of Mumbai. Then there is the flood of poor peasants from the countryside pouring into the city. We have the world's largest slums where hundreds of thousands of people survive in sub-human conditions. It is from these slums that a section of our city fathers and MLAs are drawn. What can you expect from them?'

The more I thought over the subject, the more his analysis made sense. 'What is to be done?' I asked him. 'I don't know,' he replied. 'Let's see the results of the elections,' he said, showing me the black dot on his finger to prove he had cast his vote. 'Perhaps new leaders will emerge who have no links with the underworld and are committed to restoring Mumbai to being the premier city of India.' Amen!

9 October 1999

Pakistan and us

I watched an interview of General Pervez Musharraf on the BBC. I could not believe my ears when he said more than once that in Kargil, the Pakistani army had achieved every one of its objectives and was totally successful. When he repeated the statement, he added the term *mujahideen* (holy warriors) to the victors. It sounded very odd because for weeks after the operation began, the spokesperson of the

Pakistan government denied the involvement of their army personnel in the adventure and were reluctant to accept the bodies of its soldiers killed in battle. While we claim we drove them out of our territory to the last man, General Musharraf has the cheek to tell the world that Pakistan gained a great victory in Kargil.

Once in Bombay I was invited to a reception given by the Consul General of Pakistan. Talking to some guests, I discovered the reception was in honour of the anniversary of Pakistan's victory over India in the 1965 war. I was flabbergasted. In the few weeks the war had lasted, India had occupied large parts of Pak territory and our army was close to the suburbs of Lahore when the agreement to ceasefire was signed.

In the 1971 war for the liberation of Bangladesh, Pakistani media, official and non-official, kept regaling their audiences of the great victories the Pakistani army and Air Force were achieving over us. This went on till Dhaka fell, and the abject surrender of the Pakistani army in what was East Pakistan. I would not be too surprised if after some years, Pakistanis claim that as well, as a glorious victory over India! We may well ask how much trust do the common people of Pakistan repose in the pronouncements of its civilian and military rulers?

The Pakistanis' attitudes to their rulers and changes of government are different from ours. I was in Pakistan for a few days during the rule of General Ayub Khan. I noticed no resentment against military dictatorship. Nor any great jubilation when his government fell. I was in Pakistan again during the reign of Zulfiqar Ali Bhutto. I heard a lot of stories of his profligacy, womanizing and discourtesy towards his ministers. No one did more than just gossip. I was also there when he was hanged. There was a demonstration in Rawalpindi led by women in burkhas. On the Friday following his execution, I was in Karachi, Bhutto's stamping ground. The cinemas were open and mosques were full for the *Juma namaaz*—it was as if nothing untoward had happened.

I visited Pakistan a couple of times during General Zia-ul Haq's regime. I found no signs of resentment against the dictator. When he was killed, there was no breast-beating. So it should come as no surprise that no tears were shed on Nawaz Sharif's dethroning. Nor will there be any when Pervez Musharraf gets the order of the boot on his flabby buttocks.

We Indians are the same kind of people as the Pakistanis, but our experiences of governance have been different. Save for two years of emergency rule, we have never known dictatorship. Even in those years, a large number of people including George Fernandes, Viren Shah and others carried on underground anti-government activity. The Akalis organized *satyagraha* and sent thousands of passive resisters to jail. Despite the assassinations of two prime ministers, we were able to install successive governments peacefully. However tempting it may be to exult over Pakistan's immaturity and pat our backs for having attained adult status, we must guard against complacency. Our enemies are within us: religious intolerance, lack of respect for the law, too much talk and too little action.

Editors in WPBs

A noticeable development in the small world of Indian journalism is the decline in the importance of editors and the encroachment on editorial domain by managers with the blessings of proprietors. In many newspapers, editors have been reduced to being office boys drawing large salaries, handsome expense accounts and riding chauffeur-driven cars. Editors who had illusions that papers they edited enjoyed prestige and good circulation because of their stewardship have been cut to size by their owners. Some were unceremoniously fired, some allowed to stay on to write the kind of editorials their bosses wanted: in short, editors could be crumpled up and tossed into their own WPBs (waste paper baskets).

The number of so-called editors and journalists humiliated before being kicked out of office runs into scores. They nurse their grievances over cups of coffee, but rarely have the courage to put them in print or take newspaper proprietors to court or the Press Council. Although I too have had my share of being pampered and then without courtesy shown the door, I was luckier than most in landing on my feet as a syndicated columnist.

Much more interesting than my career as a journalist is that of Vinod Mehta, currently editor of *Outlook*. I first met him when he was editing the sleazy, girlie magazine *Debonair*—the Indian version of *Playboy*—for Sushil Somani. I liked the magazine and I liked the editor. The magazine had pictures of lovely nudes and the reading material was refreshingly new. I liked the editor because he was ever-cheerful, thoroughly irreverent towards everyone, and an engaging conversationalist.

When he launched the *Sunday Observer* for Ashwin Shah of Jaico, I was happy to let him have my *Malice* column. Meanwhile, Vinod was eased out of the *Sunday Observer* and had had a brush with Ram Nath Goenka, owner of the *Indian Express*, Samir Jain, owner of the *Times of India* and Dhirubhai Ambani, till he took over as editor of the *Pioneer*, financed by L.M. Thapar. That did not last too long, and finally, he launched *Outlook* for another millionaire, Rajan Raheja. He, along with his colleague Tarun Tejpal, made it an instant success. *Outlook* is by far the most thought-provoking and readable weekly journal in the country. How long Vinod Mehta will be in his present job is anyone's guess. He is right in observing that while newspaper proprietors have to keep politicians on their side to preserve their business interests, journalists who mean to be true to their profession have to maintain an objective distance from politicians. That is the theme of Vinod Mehta's recent book, *Mr Editor, how close are you to the PM?*

23 October 1999

Mocking the law

The administration of law and justice in India has become a sick joke. Criminal cases including homicides take over ten years to come to their conclusion. Civil litigation including cases between landlords and tenants may go on for twenty years or more till one or the other party is dead. At the same time, learned jurists keep reminding us that justice delayed is justice denied. If that is so, we can assume there is no justice left in our country.

Who is responsible for this sorry state of affairs? Without doubt everyone involved: litigants, lawyers, the police and other investigative agencies, the judiciary, politicians and governments—both central and in the states. Arrears of undecided cases have reached astronomical heights and show no signs of coming down. I was hoping that our new government under A.B. Vajpayee would reverse the trend of accumulating arrears of undecided cases by devising means for speedier procedures of their disposal. Evidently, this is beyond its capabilities.

The crux of the matter is that over a dozen criminal cases pending before the courts involve the names of two former prime ministers, about a dozen former ministers of the central cabinet and one in the present cabinet, members of Parliament, half-a-dozen chief ministers and innumerable politicians. It obviously does not suit them to have cases in which they are named to be speedily concluded. They engage high-profile lawyers whose brief is to get their clients released on bail and then have hearings prolonged for as long as they can. Magistrates and judges are usually cooperative.

As sinister as big fish breaking through flimsy nets of the law is the give-and-take practised by the high and mighty. They usually belong to parties at variance with each other.

Ministers and politicians provide information against each other to investigative agencies. Their rivals do the same.

Whereas justice will require both to be brought to trial and punished, they use their clout to barter with each other: 'You don't press cases against me and I will not press cases against you.' Complete turnabouts are an essential part of the games they play. Buying over witnesses is as common as buying vegetables. If our *netas* show such disregard for law and morality, how can we expect the common people to have any respect for them?

Dog-haters and astrologers

I confess that I cannot make friends with two kinds of people: those who don't like dogs, and those who believe in astrology. Dog-haters are difficult to detect because unless forced to admit to an aversion towards canines, they keep their phobia to themselves. It is only when invited to homes of dog-lovers that they will own up by saying, 'Please put that dog in another room while I am here.' So the poor dog is chained or locked up in some other room. Dogs are in fact social creatures and hate being excluded from parties.

They bark or howl in protest. Dogs can also smell out people who do not like them and make no secret of their dislike for those who hate them. At times dog-haters conceal their dislike for dogs by taking no notice of them. But dogs being dogs are over-eager to say 'hello' to every visitor. Young dogs want to do more: they jump into the laps of visitors, lick their faces, and if repulsed, hump their legs. That should be a clear enough signal for dog-haters to depart.

Believers in astrology are a breed apart from dog-haters. While dog-haters form a miniscule minority of our population, believers in astrology form an overwhelming majority—over ninety per cent. A few you can recognize from the various rings they wear with their birth or lucky stones on them. Most are more subtle and will betray themselves by asking silly questions like 'Are you a Libra or a Scorpio?' Thereafter they will proceed to hold forth on the virtues and failings of people born under different signs of the zodiac. If I get into an argument with them, my blood pressure shoots up. They will reel off long lists of events predicted long before they occurred by famous astrologers ranging from the *Bhrighu Samhita* to Nostradamus. They will assure you that just as the moon dictates the ebb and flow of ocean tides, so different stars dictate the destinies of humans. It is not easy to catch them out as they employ delightfully vague terminology in making their predictions. On rare occasions, they are specific about the date and time of events to come and then get caught out and fall flat on their faces. I once caught Shri Madan who publishes an astrological magazine from Delhi. He made a prediction of a tragedy to take place in our Parliament on a particular day. Nothing happened. I wrote about it in my column. In reply, he abused me, calling me an ignoramus with set prejudices against his tribe.

Astrologers are in great demand before elections. Politicians run to them with their horoscopes and palms outstretched. All are assured of success; and few, very very few, make it. But it's enough to keep the myth of astral predictions alive. This last election was no different except for the fact that for the first time, our newspapers and magazines did not bother to publish astrological predictions but instead published forecasts by psephologists both before and after the votes had been cast. Not to be outdone, at least one die-hard believer in astrology was foolish enough to send me a copy of a circular letter enclosing a forecast made by a venerable astrologer whose predictions he swore by. The circular dated September 24, 1999, was from one V. Mohana who described himself as secretary of the Federal India Movement based in Chennai. After expressing anguish over the state of the nation forced to go to polls before schedule, Mohana proceeded to criticize psephologists. He wrote: 'The election has raised much din, dust and undesirable talk and practices. Speculators have been gripping the minds of the people. To top up, the exit polls have added much more confusion with regard to the outcome and result of the staggeringly phased election.'

Mohana goes on to praise the work of his organization, extolling the divine vision of their forecaster. I quote his words: 'In this milieu, when the counting starts in about a week's time, the Federal India Movement has been quietly trying to assess the outcome. In our frantic efforts to know the exact result, we have come across an accomplished astrologer Jothida Ratnam Shri D. Nagarajan who has been keeping a low profile and shuns the limelight. Sitting in one corner of Chennai, he has predicted that present Congress President Sonia Gandhi will undoubtedly lead her party to a comfortable win and form the government at the centre. After serious study and research of the planetary positions, he also asserts that whatever be the speculations, thinking, surveys or findings of exit polls, Sonia Gandhi will be the prime minister of India by early October 1999.'

The predictions of the venerable Jothida Ratnam (ruby of astrology) D. Nagarajan deserve to be quoted in full:

'I, D. Nagarajan, emphatically and categorically wish to put on record that Sonia Gandhi, President, the Indian National Congress, will lead the Congress-led front to a win with comfortable seat tally in the current Lok Sabha elections. She will form a steady Congress government at the Centre. Based on the indepth analyses and intricate calculations of the planetary placements, numerical considerations and scientific research, blended with my 'intuition' (which the Divine power has blessed me with), I also unequivocally assert that Sonia Gandhi will be the prime minister of India and will manage the governance of the country in a satisfactory manner.

'My prediction stems from the data of Sonia Gandhi's name value, star, *rasi,* planetary placements, the number arrangements, her compatibility of numbers with respect to others, details of the party and the Indian National Congress, the serial number of Lok Sabha, the date of announcement of the elections, the date of counting of the votes.

'My findings and predictions were ready a few weeks back. But I withheld the same for specific reasons till the fag end of the polls and a few days prior to the counting. I have pitched the timings of revelation till this day. I have also predicted the apt and beneficial date and time for formation of the ministry, oath-taking etc. and will reveal the same shortly.

'It will not be out of place if I add that I have devoted my life to the study of astrology and scored success and accuracy for all my predictions. I had predicted the success of US Presidents like Nixon, Jimmy Carter and currently Bill Clinton. I am confident that the success of Sonia Gandhi and her becoming the prime minister of India, is a foregone conclusion.'

Incidentally, the forecast made at the same time by my friend Bhaskara Rao who runs the Centre for Media Studies was very close to the actual results for the Lok Sabha and the three states which went to the polls (except in the case of Uttar Pradesh in which he admits to miscalculations). His forecasts were published in *Outlook*.

Isn't it time we erased words like *Rahukal, Yamagand, Gulikakal* and all the mumbo-jumbo of astrological and *vaastu* vocabulary from our lexicon? They do not become a nation committed to developing a scientific temperament.

13 November 1999

Ugly Indian of the new millennium

Come autumn, most clubs have their annual
elections. For every place on the executive
committee, secretary, Vice-President and
President, there are usually four or five
candidates. The more prestigious the club,
the more vulgar its electioneering process.
Months before the date of casting votes, come
invitations to cocktail parties and dinners
where the merits of aspirants are served along
with whiskey and kebabs. When Scotch was in
short supply, I used to accept these invitations
but never went to vote.

Once I was bullied into putting my name
up for election by a group of do-gooders who
wanted to throw out men and women who had
made it a practice to stand for elections every
year and run the club by extending patronage
for personal profit. Candidates put up by the
do-gooders including myself, were elected with
thumping majorities. However, we were not
able to change the atmosphere of the club. The
year following it was the same: cocktail parties,
printed letters extolling virtues of aspirants,
women shamelessly begging for votes for

their husbands. On election nights, lines of cars outside the Gymkhana and the Golf Club extended over 200 yards on each side.

I have reason to believe the same happens in most well-known clubs in Kolkata, Mumbai and Chennai. Our cities have new names, but their citizens have not changed in their habits. If the rich, educated, urban elite hunger for petty posts in the governing bodies of clubs, is it surprising that for every panchayat, zilla parishad, Vidhan Sabha and Parliament seat, there are dozens of aspirants and everyone elected wants to be a *pradhan* or cabinet minister no matter how many parties he has to ditch, how many colleagues he or she has to stab in the back?

We have always been a nation of self-seeking sycophants. This national characteristic has assumed epidemic proportions. We are stricken with the disease of *Chaudharis*—everyone wants to be the leader of his area. The pretence is always the same: 'I want to serve the people.' Never before have the words 'social service' been as prostituted as they are today. What hope is there for our country as it enters the new millennium?

A nation of litterbugs

There was a time when Lodhi Park was the
most scenic in the country: half-a-dozen
ancient mosques, mausolea and a stone bridge
spread over sprawling acres of green lawns,
flowering trees and an enclosed garden full of
exotic varieties of roses. During the summer
months, the fragrance of *maulsari* spread
everywhere. The park was rich with bird and
animal life. At one time, partridges, peacocks
and wild hares scampered around the bushes.
During the Raj days, a cinder track ran round
the park on which *sahib log* both white and
brown, exercised their horses.

For some years after Independence, valiant
attempts were made to enhance the beauty of
the park. The moat around Sikander Lodhi's
tomb was filled with water, and a fountain
in its midst sprouted a jet of water over fifty
feet in the air. The park was kept scrupulously
clean, the lawns kept evergreen with sprinklers
spraying clean water on them and mowed
regularly. I took my evening walks in the park.
It was the favourite place of Simba my Alsatian
who loved running alongside the car over the

ancient bridge into the car park in the centre. Occasionally he scented a hare or a peacock and chased it till he was out of breath. When Simba died, I stopped going to the park. Apart from losing my companion, I found far too many people about to be able to spend a quiet evening all by myself.

After a lapse of many years, I have resumed taking my evening walks in Lodhi Park. Many changes have taken place. All its four entrances are clogged with cars. That is to be expected, as the number of walkers has gone up by the thousands. Partridges, peacocks and hares have vanished. So have many birds. Now, only crows, pigeons and mynahs are seen.

The moat is almost always dry or covered with green slime in which even frogs can't survive. The fountain no longer sprouts a jet of water and the lawns are watered with water that is unfiltered. The stench of sewage is all-pervasive. Hordes of picnickers throng the park on holidays and leave paper plates, plastic tumblers and plates strewn all over the lawns.

Metal containers meant for garbage, bearing the signs 'use me', are not used. Nobody comes to clear the litter. For days on end I have sat on the steps of an old mosque facing the same crumpled remains of plastic water bottles and empty bags of potato chips. A dozen *khomchawalas* selling ingredients for bhelpuri do the rounds. Their patrons leave empty leaf cups all over. Without doubt, most people who come to the park belong to the educated, upper class. Parents don't tell their children that littering is unsocial and unhygienic. School teachers don't bother to tell students that garbage should be deposited in garbage bins.

Anywhere else in the world, a person throwing a cigarette butt or an empty match box in a public place would be immediately arrested and fined. But not in what was once one of the most beautiful parks in the world. Virtually the only part of Lodhi Gardens still left free is the stone-paved path which runs round it. It is no longer safe for people of my age who walk slowly. Young men go round at breakneck speed; young girls with big bosoms and fat behinds jog past swaying their arms wildly. For the old, it is only a few benches or steps of old buildings to sit on and brood over days gone by.

I do not know who is in charge of Lodhi Gardens. If it is the Archaeological Department, it is doing a very shoddy job of repairing old monuments. (Ancient walls have been plastered over with light yellow plaster that robs it of its antiquity.) It is also responsible for the upkeep of the lawns. Apparently, clearing litter is not one of its responsibilities.

4 December 1999

Thumbs up, thumbs down

In ancient Rome, warriors fought against each other in public arenas. When one fell down, the victor looked up to the spectators for their final verdict. If they wanted the defeated man's life to be spared, they pointed their thumbs upwards; if they wanted him to be killed, they pointed their thumbs downwards. The practice has continued in our times: when we want to wish someone good luck, we give him the thumbs up sign; when we want someone to be destroyed, we give them thumbs down.

On my own I indulge in the thumbs-up, thumbs-down game with our politicians. A few I usually give thumbs up no matter what party they belong to. In this category are men like Atal Behari Vajpayee, Jyoti Basu, Chandrababu Naidu, Digvijay Singh, R.K. Hegde, Madhavrao Scindia, Manmohan Singh, Mamata Banerjee, Rajesh Pilot, Madhu Dandavate, Bansi Lal and a few others. What they have in common is their positive approach to problems; they are builders, not destroyers. They are also clean and honest; they do not lie.

The thumbs-down list is much longer and keeps on getting longer. All whom I suspect had a hand in the killing of Sikhs in 1984, the destruction of the Babri Masjid in 1992, and the anti-Muslim violence that followed, I automatically put in this category along with Bal Thackeray and Ashok Singhal who head the list. I also put unprincipled party-ditchers like Sharad Pawar, Buta Singh and S.S. Ahluwalia with them. Their approach to problems is negative; they are breakers, not builders.

High on my thumbs-down list is Kalyan Singh, erstwhile chief minister of Uttar Pradesh. He has many minus points against him: a hand in the destruction of the Masjid, stabbing his party boss and his party in the back, arousing communal passions again over building a Ram mandir on the site of a demolished place of worship. We do not have to turn our thumbs down on a character like Kalyan Singh; he is the victim of hubris and author of his own political hara-kiri. There are far too many of his ilk around us. The sooner they eliminate themselves from the political arena, the better it will be for the nation.

18 December 1999

Farewell to 1999

In the last week of the year, I go over my diary to refresh my memory of what I have done in the past twelve months. My diary is fairly detailed: I write about the weather, trees, migratory birds and butterflies, people who came to see me, parties I attended, scores of tennis sets I played, India's showing in international sports. The last items are devoted to political upheavals, earthquakes, cyclones, air and rail disasters, murders, miscarriages of justice and so on. It gives me a fair idea of what the world, India and I went through in the year.

January began on a grim note. Smog in the mornings, flights delayed, every third person down with viral fever, most people coughing and spitting phlegm. Three ghastly murders took place in the space of one day: that of the sprightly newspaper reporter Shivani Bhatnagar in Delhi and those of the Australian missionary Staines and his two sons in Orissa. Shivani's killer remains untracked. Of the Staines killers said to be members of a Bajrang Dal gang, the leader, Dara Singh, is still absconding.

In February, three eminent men died. Ashok Jain, chairman of the *Times of India* group died of cancer in America. He was at one time my employer and later sacked me without ceremony. The wonderful thing about the Jains is that they do not mourn death but regard it as a cause of celebration. So no fuss was made over Ashok Jain's departure. On the other hand, the demise of King Hussein of Jordan was turned into an international event with the heads of many States attending the funeral. The third to go was General Sundarji,

controversial commander of 'Operation Blue
Star', who often promised to write his version of
the tragic episode but never got down to doing
so. However, the legacy of mismanagement of
the Golden Temple took a decisive turn with
a split in the Akali party with Badal heading
the majority group against Tohra who had
reigned supreme for twenty-five years. Badal
sacked Bhai Ranjit Singh, nominated by
Tohra as *jathedar* of the Akal Takht. He also
appointed Bibi Jagir Kaur, the first woman to
head the SGPC. The Badal-Tohra split was
to have disastrous consequences for Akalis of
both factions.

March saw the demise of Yehudi Menuhin,
the greatest violin maestro of our times; a friend
of the Nehrus and India. An IAF transport plane
crashed near Palam airport killing twenty-
three; a *jhuggi-jhopri* fire near Vijayghat took
fifty lives, and in Bihar, confrontation between
Ranvir Sena (landowning militia) and Naxalites
resulted in scores of vendetta killings.

For April I have only two items of
national interest—the rest are cricket matches
with India levelling scores with Pakistan and
getting the better of England at Sharjah.

Of importance to the Sikhs were the 300th anniversary of the Foundation of the Khalsa Panth at Anandpur Sahib. I have never seen a larger gathering of Khalsas in my life—there must have been about thirty lakh present. Less cheerful was the defeat of Vajpayee's government by one vote, for no reason that made any sense to me except political chicanery. The country was plunged into unnecessary general elections with Vajpayee assured of a massive sympathy vote.

It is hard to fathom the reasons why Pakistan decided to indulge in military adventurism against India. In February, Prime Minister Vajpayee had gone by bus to Lahore on a goodwill mission and extended a hand of friendship to the people. Unknown to us, by then, Pakistani army units and foreign mercenaries hired by them or financed by Osama bin Laden had surreptitiously occupied bunkers on snow-bound heights built by our army and vacated for the winter months.

Our intelligence had obviously failed: we had to pay a very heavy price for its failure. It took our army and air force two months to drive the Pakistani infiltrators out of our soil.

As one would have expected, Vajpayee came to be looked upon as the saviour of India. And in Pakistan, the civilian-elected government of Nawaz Sharif began to be looked upon with suspicion by the Pakistani army topbrass, for bringing the disgrace of defeat on their country. The one cheerful item of news during the bloody confrontations was Leander Paes and Mahesh Bhupati winning the French Open and the Wimbledon men's finals. Never before had India attained such heights in the game.

While we became insensitive to the killings of innocents by terrorists in Kashmir, Bihar, Orissa, Assam and Andhra Pradesh, the passing of eminent men left a deeper sense of loss. Hakim Abdul Hamid, founder of Hamdard and the university of the same name, a good God-fearing man, died in the end of July. He was followed a week later by Nirad C. Chaudhuri, who died in Oxford at the age of 101. Reviled by his countrymen all his life, he was paid handsome tributes by his traducers in every journal of the country. Meanwhile, people of lesser renown fell victim to man-made disaster: 400 were killed in a head-on collision between two trains in Bengal. An earthquake near Izmir

(Turkey) accounted for 50,000, followed by another in Taiwan that killed over 2000.

By the first week of October, all the results of the general elections had been announced. The BJP and its allies won a comfortable majority over its chief rival, the Congress, which was reduced to its lowest-ever representation. It did do well in some states however, including Uttar Pradesh, which caused much heartburn in ruling party circles. It was forced to expel Kalyan Singh, as committed a Hindu communalist as any, who threatened to humble Vajpayee, raised the Ram mandir issue in Ayodhya no matter what the courts had to say on the subject. Kalyan or no Kalyan, Vajpayee was back in the saddle firmer than ever before.

Though I have strong reservations against many of his colleagues and allies who keep on fooling the people with garbled phraseology of the 'Mandir not being on their agenda', I have a gut feeling that Vajpayee has shed the khaki-knicker mentality and become a world statesman with a broad vision. He has also rid himself of trouble-making allies like Jayalalitha, and should be able to give the country a stable government for five years. His first challenge came when a cyclone of unprecedented fury struck the Orissa coastline, taking about 30,000 lives. This was followed by a flood in Venezuela which took over 50,000. Such God-made disasters make me question those believers who claim that God is not only all-powerful but also just and merciful. Would all these holy men who spout *pravachans* on various TV channels and write columns in daily papers, answer simple question like the one I have posed?

Early last month went two eminent industrialists—Harish Mahendra and Darbari Seth. Darbari had a passion for Urdu ghazals. One night we sat up till 3 a.m. listening to Mehdi Hasan on one of his visits to Bombay.

While thousands of victims of the Orissa cyclone were still untracked, Bihar and UP celebrated two weddings on a regal scale. Laloo Yadav and Rabri Devi for their daughter, and Mulayam Singh Yadav for his son, organized receptions as princely families of yesteryear used to do. These are self-proclaimed leaders of the poor and downtrodden, and have no doubt exhorted their followers not to waste

money on marriages. So must have Jayalalitha
in her innumerable election campaigns. They
are by no means the only three to preach one
thing and practice another. More painful is
the fact that leaders of all parties, including
Communists, attended these vulgar displays of
unearned wealth. The only words I can think
of using for them are *besharam* and *beyhaya*—
without shame and without propriety.

The year came to a tragic end with the
hijacking of an Indian Airlines plane from
Kathmandu to Delhi with 189 passengers
aboard. It was the saddest Christmas I have
ever had which was spent alternating between
outbursts of anger and tears. What kind of
security checks the Kathmandu airport police
and Indian Airlines carry out before passengers
boarded the aircraft can be gauged from the fact
that five heavily-armed men were cleared. Why
was the aircraft allowed to leave Amritsar? The
nightmare will haunt everyone for many nights.

Last of all, I speak of myself. 1999 brought
me a bumper of awards and an honorary
doctorate. My last novel, *The Company of
Women,* which I did not rate very high myself
and was panned by literary critics, remained on

top of India's bestseller list for over four months.
To hell with critics; long live my readers! I wish
them good health and prosperity.

1 January 2000

Biased media

There was a time, not so long ago, when if
anything went wrong in the country, our
netas and following them our *patrakars*,
immediately put the blame on America's CIA.
If you dared to question them on their sources
of information, they promptly dubbed you 'a
Washington patriot'.

The CIA has now become *neta*- and media-
friendly. It has been replaced by Pakistan's ISI.
There can be little doubt that this agency has a
lot to do with sustaining anti-Indian terrorism
in Kashmir, Punjab and elsewhere, but the way
our politicians and the press portray it as the
source of all mischief that takes place in our
country—communal riots, fake currency notes,
bomb blasts etc.—it gives ISI more credit for
mischief-making than it is capable of.

It is much the same in Pakistan. All that goes wrong is promptly ascribed to our secret agency, RAW. What Pakistani politicians, its state-controlled radio and TV and a section of their press have to say about RAW is highly complimentary but hardly believable. However, both ISI and RAW are used in our countries to keep already existing ill-will at fever pitch. I am sure if anything happened to people like Kuldip Nayyar or me (who are periodically condemned for pleading for friendlier relations with Pakistan), RAW would hold the ISI responsible, and the ISI would claim that it was done by RAW just to give ISI a bad name.

This kind of mud-slinging would be comic if it was not tragic. It is unworthy of the media of both our countries, particularly ours which claims to be entirely free of meddling by the State. Our print and electronic media must not rely so much on Government handouts, wire services and foreign media.

This brings me to a disgraceful instance of reckless irresponsibility in reporting, committed recently by two independent TV channels which, following every newscast, claim to being free, unbiased, objective and based on experience.

When the first news of the hijacking of our plane from Kathmandu to Kandahar was reported, following perhaps a report in the *Washington Post,* both these channels said that the hijackers were Sikhs. The *Washington Post* was quick to correct its error, and apologize for it. However, neither of our TV channels that made this blunder bothered to do so, despite the many protests sent to them. They should have known that naming a community for a criminal act committed by one of its members is unethical and can have dangerous repercussions. Not only did these channels get their facts wrong and transgress the unwritten code of news broadcasting, but they refused to express regret for having done so. Now what should we make of their self-righteous claims to truthfulness, objectivity and experience?

5 February 2000

Down with bigotry

The most disturbing feature of present-day India is the growing spirit of intolerance—

religious, social and cultural. The blame can be laid squarely on the resurgence of religious fundamentalism among all communities save Christians and Parsis. Semi-literate *mahants,* mullahs and *granthis* take it upon themselves to decide what is good and what is not good for the country. Opportunist politicians bray their support. And if they happen to be in positions of power, they impose their will on others regardless of their legal rights.

So *hukamnamas,* fatwas and denunciations flow from the mouths of people who have little concern for the democratic rights of others and even less respect for the law of the land. They are enemies of India; a contemptible lot. It is the duty of the administration, be it of the central or the state governments, to restrain them, detain them, take them to court and punish them. It is also the duty of citizens to confront them on public platforms and in the streets and try to knock some sense into them.

The fate of Deepa Mehta's film *Water* is the latest instance of religious bigots getting away with murder because the authorities failed in their duty to curb them. The film script was okayed by the Ministry of Information and

Broadcasting. Thereafter, it was the duty of the Ministry to see that no one was allowed to obstruct the shooting. And if anyone did, the duty of the Home Ministry was to arrest them and bring them to trial. As it transpired, the state government let vandals get away with it.

Nothing better could have been expected from the waffly chief minister of Uttar Pradesh whose left hand does not know what his right hand is doing, and who describes the destruction of the Babri Masjid as a peaceful occurrence. It was a good opportunity for the Vajpayee government, chiefly Home Minister L.K. Advani, to act swiftly and come down with an iron hand on lawbreakers. However, both the state and the central government failed miserably in maintaining law and order. It is a shame that Deepa Mehta had to amend her own script approved by the I&B Minister to pander to the view of the *pandas* of Varanasi.

The basic role of a democracy is respect for the opinions of people who differ with you. No one is entitled to thrust his views on others. Banning or burning books, films or paintings is medieval barbarism. If you dislike what you have heard about a book, don't read it. If you

don't approve of a film, don't go to watch it.
If you don't like a painter or the themes of his
paintings, don't see them. But in a cultured
society, you have no right to prevent others
from reading those books or seeing those films
or paintings. It is as simple as that.

12 February 2000

Religion to serve the people

Many readers accuse me of harbouring anti-
religious sentiments. That is not correct.
I respect all religions as well as people who
subscribe to them. My grouse is that all religions
as practised in India today have become time-
wasting exercises that do not benefit society nor
make an individual a better human being. No
people on earth spend so much time in prayer,
meditation, rituals, pilgrimages and listening to
so-called spiritual discourses as we Indians do.
Nor do any other people enjoy as many religious
holidays. For a country left far behind others in
the race for prosperity, this pattern of behaviour
must change, and the sooner the better.

Religious institutions and preachers can be very effective in solving our nation's problems provided they shed their traditional roles of only performing rituals and singing bhajans. It will be hard for them as they have vested interests in doing what they have always been doing—ringing bells, chanting mantras, singing hymns and getting paid for it. Their activities do not benefit society in any way. I make bold to make the following suggestions:

No place of worship should be granted land or permission to build on unless it has provision for a primary school and teaching staff to go with it.

No priest should perform the sacred thread, *amrit* or marriage ceremonies of boys and girls unless he is assured they have studied up to the tenth standard.

At every marriage ceremony, the priest should make the marrying couple take an oath that on the birth of their second child, both will voluntarily undergo sterilization.

Hindu and Sikh priests should inform people that there is nothing in their religions which forbids the disposal of the dead by burial under the earth or in the sea. They should emphasize that killing a living tree to use its wood to get rid of corpses is an irreligious act. Local authorities should provide space close to all towns and villages where the Hindu and Sikh dead can be buried. No monuments may be built on their graves. Only a tree may be planted to mark the site or the land be returned to agriculture every five years. Many Hindu communities of the south bury their dead; many eminent Hindu leaders including Swami Chinmayananda were buried in recent years.

Preachers of religion must emphasize the value of working and earning one's own livelihood. Guru Nanak made work an article of Sikh faith: *Kirat karo* (work), *vand chakho* (share what you earn), *naam japo* (take the name of the Lord). Note the order of priorities— work comes first, charity and prayer come later. It is from his teachings that I have coined the slogan for modern India: Work is worship, but worship is not work.

27 February 2000

The Comeback Kid

Everyone had written him off as a political washout—rival politicians, poll forecasters, print media, television channels, expert psephologists, the lot. Laloo has proved beyond a shadow of doubt that the entire bunch of self-proclaimed analysts of Indian political trends are no more than a bunch of *bewakoofs*. Only one man, Shahir Hassan, a Bihari, who had toured his home state before the elections and has been working with Sitaram Kesri for many years, told me, 'Don't write off Laloo Yadav. He has a strong hold on the lower castes and Muslims who can sway the elections in his favour.' I did not believe him then. Now I do. I also do not believe the explanations now being given by soured losers as to how and why Laloo got the better of them. It was not the misalliance of disparate parties, not divisions in their ranks, not the lack of campaigning nor the absence of national leaders (Atal Behari Vajpayee, Sonia Gandhi and George Fernandes were there). I am convinced it was Laloo's one-man army that won the battle of the hustings in many parts of Bihar. In India, we can't ignore the role of charismatic leaders in winning elections.

What would the Bharatiya Janata Party be without Atal Behari Vajpayee's powerful oratory? However, his appeal is limited to urban areas where people can appreciate his *shudh* high-falutin Hindi. Not so in the case of Laloo Yadav. He's every bit as good an orator as Atalji, but scores over him by speaking in rustic Bihari dialect (which even Bihar-*putra* Shatrughan Sinha cannot match). He is not inhibited in the use of earthy, often abusive language which endears him to the poor illiterate masses.

They admire his arrogance, the way he walks with his head held high, his chest puffed out: he is like a bantam cock strutting onto an arena. They like his assumptions of leadership: he always uses the royal plural 'We' (*hum*) for himself, never the humble 'I' (*mein*). He is every inch the *badshah* of Bihar—poor Biharis acknowledge him as their monarch. They overlook the innumerable criminal charges of misfeasance (including appropriating money meant to buy cattle fodder), as something his enemies had foisted on him; they ignore the criticism that he paid no heed to family planning norms himself by having Rabri Devi bear him nine children, or about having put her on the throne when he was in goal, knowing full well that she was unfit to be chief minister.

They did mind his squandering money at his daughter's marriage. But in their way of looking at things, kings are not bound by laws that apply to common folk. This may sound like an over-simplified explanation for the results of the elections in Bihar. It is not: the days of charismatic leaders with gifted tongues are not over.

I saw the resurgence of Gorkha pride under the leadership of Subhas Ghising. I see it in Laloo's Bihar and in the BJP's rise to pre-eminence under Mr Vajpayee. Without men like them at the helm, their parties would collapse like deflated balloons.

11 March 2000

Hometown Delhi

If familiarity breeds contempt between humans, it works the other way when it comes to the village, town or city in which one was born and brought up. See the passion with which Calcuttans love their Kolkata, Bombaikars love their Mumbai and Madrasis love their Chennai.

These three metropolises have little to boast about their ancestry or historical buildings, parks, or quality of life: they are congested, squalid and, to the outsider, unliveable. By contrast, Delhi has a hoary past, ancient and modern buildings of great architectural merit, beautiful parks and gardens.

There are good reasons for Dilliwalas to love their Delhi: Indraprastha, Shahjahanabad (nee Dilli). The only minus point about the citizens of the capital is that the majority of them have not yet developed a sense of pride for belonging to it. Most of them are refugees from Pakistan who have yet to put their roots in Delhi's soil, and continue to have nostalgic memories of their Punjabi homeland. Then there are civil servants from different parts of India who want to get back to wherever they came from.

Delhi has paid dearly for letting in people with no sense of belonging to it, and allowing them to smother many of its ancient and noble ruins with new housing colonies and slums. All the *jhuggi-jhopris* that have erupted like cancerous sores in and around the city are gifts of ambitious Punjabi *mohajir* politicians who wanted to create vote banks for themselves. They did so with a total lack of concern for the future of the city. Future generations of Dilliwalas will never forget them for their criminality.

25 March 2000

Scan QR code to access the
Penguin Random House India website